Nikki Logan lives next to a string of protected wetlands in Western Australia, with her long-suffering partner and a menagerie of furred, feathered and scaly mates. She studied film and theater at university, and worked for years in advertising and film distribution before finally settling down in the wildlife industry. Her romance with nature goes way back, and she considers her life charmed, given that she works with wildlife by day and writes fiction by night—the perfect way to combine her two loves. Nikki believes that the passion and risk of falling in love are perfectly mirrored in the danger and beauty of wild places. Every romance she writes contains an element of nature, and if readers catch a waft of rich earth or the spray of wild ocean between the pages she knows her job is done. Visit Nikki at her Web site, www.nikkilogan.com.au.

To Mum, whose passion for anything printed
rubbed off on me from an early age.

Thank you to The Bootcampers—I may have been the first across the line, but I know I won't be the last. Many thanks also to Melissa(s) James and Smith for your advice and encouragement, to Kim Young for trusting my voice more than I did and to the beautiful Rachel Bailey for... pretty much everything else. You may never know what a pivotal part you played in the realization of my dream.

And to Pete—who's picked up the slack of a woman working two jobs, and grown accustomed to the back of my head and to eating dinner solo—you *are* my hero (sorry about all the vacuuming).

NIKKI LOGAN

Lights, Camera...
Kiss the Boss

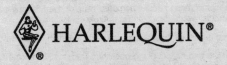

TORONTO • NEW YORK • LONDON
AMSTERDAM • PARIS • SYDNEY • HAMBURG
STOCKHOLM • ATHENS • TOKYO • MILAN • MADRID
PRAGUE • WARSAW • BUDAPEST • AUCKLAND

Recycling programs
for this product may
not exist in your area.

ISBN-13: 978-0-373-17642-7

LIGHTS, CAMERA...KISS THE BOSS

First North American Publication 2010.

Copyright © 2009 by Nikki Logan.

www.eHarlequin.com

Printed in U.S.A.

A special bonus from Nikki…
Nikki's Urban Gardening Tips

*"To forget how to dig the earth
and to tend the soil is to forget ourselves."*
—Gandhi

I adore images of past civilizations being reclaimed by nature—giant octopus-tentacle roots creeping out over a tumbled building; vines tangling down over what were once proud arches; determined trees emerging through cracked stone to stretch to the heavens. They reinforce the concept of the tenacity and resilience of nature.

Why should we wait for our civilization to die out before letting nature back in? Plants are the lungs of a city; they reduce air pollution, absorb radiant heat, insulate, improve aesthetics, protect and feed wildlife, and give humans somewhere to recreate and recharge the spiritual batteries. Unlike their rural counterparts, urban gardens face challenges such as increased exposure (to wind, sun and frost), radiant heat amplified by tiling, glazing and altitude and, most of all, limited space. But it is possible to integrate built and natural environments, and there are many ways to create a resource-effective, attractive or useful piece of *urban nature* no matter where you live.

Here are my tips:

- **Rooftop Gardens** are best created on flat open surfaces and best suited to the types of plants that like a lot of sunlight/exposure (unless your rooftop is dwarfed by giant towers all around). You can create sunken mazes through *giant planters* full of exposure-tolerant species, communal *vegetable and herb gardens* (veggies love sunlight and neighbors love free veggies!), *hydroponic* gardens (a true DIY project!), or unique alien-looking forest *xenoscapes* made from giant succulents and cacti. Better yet, by using plants that are indigenous to your area, you will provide habitat, food sources, shelter and possible nest sites for local wildlife *(flora for fauna)*. Plant thickly and abundantly (as nature does) and the wildlife will love you.

- **Balconies/Terraces/Courtyards** are perfect for smaller, smarter gardens. *Planters and pots* (on ground or hanging from patios) give you heaps of scope for themed, colorful, eye-catching gardens that can change regularly (nature is definitely not static). *Wall gardens* will have color and fragrance climbing your walls or tumbling down it. A *vertical garden* is the new kid on the urban-garden block and simulates the way plants grow in perilous cliff-face situations, seeming to practically live on air. You need a specially created hydroponic wall-mounting system, but once set up they are extremely cost- and water-effective. Imagine your building growing lichen, epiphytes and mosses. Beautiful and natural use of "dead" space.

- For those with **no outdoor space at all** (poor you!) the ancient art of *bonsai* can create miniature forests in well-lit locations, while an array of *indoor plants* helps bring the outside in (with some planning and care). *Water plants* need no maintenance and are hard to kill as long as they live in a water feature near some natural light. Or if you have absolutely no green thumb whatsoever, how about a *garden in a vase*—displaying plant cuttings with interesting shapes, colors and textures, lichens or seed masses in seasons when flowers aren't abundant. Get creative with colors, pots and themes and use lots of them to surround yourself with the smells and look of nature.

CHAPTER ONE

'IS THAT even legal?'

Ava Lange glared at the row of suited clones flanking Daniel Arnot in his high-rise Sydney office. Smugness fattened their expressions; they were all too used to getting their own way.

Four against one. *Nice.*

'Can they do this, Dan? Mid-contract?' Her use of *they* was no accident. The word demarcated a battlefield, with the network suits on one side and her on the other. Between them stretched a mile of barbed tangles—a very apt representation of Ava's feelings towards all of them right now. Particularly the man in the centre, whose fringed brown eyes stared steadily back at her.

'We can, Ava, yes.'

Ah.

Disappointment bit deep as Daniel declared his allegiance. Then anger surged in like a king wave, swamping any anxiety she had about being called in today. She'd assumed she was here to be fired, not promoted.

The former held vastly more appeal.

She stalled her hands before they smacked down on his desk, settling them instead with deceptive care. Blessedly, they were steady. 'You're telling me keeping my job as landscape consultant for *Urban Nature* is now conditional on me getting in front of the camera?'

Clone Number One eagerly spoke up. 'There is provision in your contract for AusOne to modify the manner in which you—'

Dan looked askance at the man until he fell silent, then he turned and reclaimed her gaze steadily. 'Test audiences loved your brief appearance on the behind-the-scenes episode last season,' Dan said, as though that explained it all. 'We'd like to give you a fly and see what happens.'

It had been a long time since she'd last swum in the chocolatey depths of his eyes. Ava had to steel herself against the urge. 'I have no interest in being on television.'

His jaw tightened, and some perverse part of her delighted to know she was troubling him. That she was impacting on him at all. But he wasn't done yet; those eyes were at their blankest when that mind was working its hardest.

'Ava, this is a once-in-a-lifetime opportunity,' he said. 'You should take it.'

She pulled her hands off the polished surface of his desk, leaving a heat-aura in the shape of her slender fingers. It evaporated into nothing, along with her words in the face of Dan's blind determination to get his way. Her pulse picked up and she straightened.

'I have *no interest* in being on television, Dan. I'm saying no.'

Clone Number One piped up again. 'You can't say no. You're contracted.'

Ava's eyes flicked to him, to see how serious he was about that. He had the intense look of a feral dog scenting blood. Ava imagined just how rabid he'd be in court, and how many prize horses her father would have to sell to help her mount a legal defence. She swallowed the discomfort.

Seasoned leather protested as Dan settled his surfer's shoulders deeper into his chair. He silently lifted two fingers and all three lawyers rose as one. If she hadn't been so furious, Ava might have laughed.

She kept her eyes fixed on Dan's dark brown ones as the

clones filed past her to the door. It was only when his posture changed that she knew they were alone. He ran a carefully manicured hand through his hundred-dollar haircut.

Manicures, Dan? Really? The Daniel Arnot she remembered had paid about as little attention to his cuticles as he had to politics. If he couldn't surf it, he couldn't see it. As a girl, she'd dreamed he'd turn that singular focus in her direction—just once. Now he had, she wanted to bolt from the room.

He looked at her from beneath an untroubled brow. 'Ava...'

'Don't!' She shot to her feet, recognising that honey-smooth tone all too well. He'd used it on her half his life when he wanted something. Today was not the day to discover whether or not it still had power over her. She prowled across his office, venting a warning over her shoulder. 'I know where this is going. You sharpened your negotiation skills on me and my brother growing up, remember?'

'Ava, if you say no you'll be breaking your contract with the network and the piranhas waiting outside will pull you to pieces in court. Is that what you want?'

A horribly expensive and public legal case? That was the exact opposite of what she wanted. She just wanted to grow her consultancy business and build herself some kind of financial security. Right now she couldn't afford to fight, or the bad publicity. Heck, she could barely afford the taxi fare to this meeting! Every cent she earned these days she plunged into her business.

She made a beeline for the ornamental black bamboo in the corner, where it was strangled in its constricting pot. Its roots had nowhere to go.

I can empathise entirely.

She spun around, thick hair swinging. 'Don't you know me at all, Dan? What made you think I'd go for this?'

'Common sense. You don't have a whole lot of options here, Ava.'

Irritation hissed out of her and she crossed towards him. 'I enjoy my job the way it is: behind-the-scenes, designing the gardens, planning the themes.'

'You'll still get to do all that; you'll just be doing it on camera. A handful of set-ups per shoot and the rest is unchanged.' He rubbed his chin and Ava lost her train of thought for a moment, suddenly imagining it was *her* palm tracing over the stubble growing along the square angles of his jaw.

She shook her head and doubled her focus. 'Except that I'll be on set all the time, instead of in my home office working on the designs.'

Long fingers waved her concern away. 'We'll get you a mobile office.'

The speed with which he offered a six-figure sweetener took her aback. His cashed-up world was a million miles from her carefully budgeted one, but even so it was suspiciously generous. She sank onto one hip and tipped her head to study him.

'What's in this for you?' His jaw set and she knew she was onto something. 'You know I'd never go for something which puts me right in the public eye. So what is it, Dan? Why the pressure?'

'Ava...' *There it was again—that tone.* 'Be reasonable.'

Heat roared through her body. 'You're asking me to give up my home, my business and my life to give you what you want. I think I have a right to know what you're getting out of it. Money? Promotion? A corner office?'

That one hit home. A tic flared in his left eye, but he didn't bite. 'One season, Ava. Thirteen shows. Then your contract expires and you can negotiate freely.'

She snorted. The last time she'd been free had been six months ago, right before she'd signed on with AusOne. Back then, the promise of a year's fixed income and the chance to quadruple her portfolio had been like a siren's song. And it had been going to plan for the most part.

But *this*... After everything her family had done for him. What had happened to him?

Fury and a healthy dose of Lange mulishness made her rash.

'This is hardly a negotiation. I wonder what my father would have to say about you press-ganging me into this.'

Like a disturbed tiger snake he shot out of his chair and advanced around the desk, stopping a mere breath away from her. Ava met his stare and filtered air in and out through her lips rather than risk inhaling his intoxicating scent.

Nine years had changed nothing.

'He'd say *Thank you, Dan, for making sure Ava's livelihood is secure—that she has food in the fridge and a future in the industry she loves.*' Brown eyes turned nearly black as he glared down at her. 'Not to mention for the extraordinary boost the publicity will give your business.'

He radiated furious warmth, and Ava had to force herself not to bask in it. Not to look at him and think about how well the extra nine years suited him. 'I don't value the publicity and I don't consider hosting a gardening show will do diddly to help my career—my *serious* career—in landscape design. Quite the opposite, in fact.'

Colour streaked along those sensational cheekbones. 'This would be the same gardening show that has bankrolled your fledgling consultancy, yes? A show you obviously have little respect for.'

Guilt intensified her heat. She'd used his television programme to kick-start her business and they both knew it. Being a hypocrite didn't sit well with her. She'd always prided herself on her honesty, too. *Curse him!*

'You might as well put me in a bikini and drape me over an expensive car,' she said. Heat flared in his eyes before they dulled to blank, behind-the-desk Dan. 'How many people do you suppose will want to commission me to design their corporate landscaping projects if I'm a poster-girl for television? You're bargaining with my professional self-respect.'

Conscious of her shaking voice, she bought some calm-down time by filling a glass with cool water from an ornate pitcher and taking a long, slow sip. Then she crossed the thick wool carpet and emptied the remainder onto the parched bamboo. The hint of a smile on his face when she glanced at him sent her roaring straight back up the Richter scale to furious.

'What?' she snapped.

'You love your plants. It's part of who you are.' Sincerity glittered in his eyes. 'Why not let that enthusiasm and expertise show for everyone to see? No more getting irritated when a presenter mispronounces the Latin or dumps a plant into unprepared soil. You virtually write the scripts anyway—why not simply be the one to deliver them?'

She narrowed her eyes, thinking furiously. She was trapped by her contract; the lawyers knew it and Dan knew it. They were just waiting for her to catch on. There was no way in the world she would be able to match one of Australia's biggest television networks legally, and neither could she afford to resign. In fact, the pay rise Dan was offering meant she could wash her hands of AusOne at the end of her contract and still be on track with her business plan.

Just six months.

'Ava, they have you over a barrel. You really don't have a choice here.'

Her head snapped up. No way was she going to cave just because she couldn't afford a five-hundred-dollar-an-hour lawyer. The days of her just giving in to Daniel Arnot were well and truly over.

'I get to be hands-on,' she said. 'No swanning in for two shots and then leaving assistants to do all the work...'

'Fine. But not at the expense of your designing,' he countered.

'Naturally. And Shannon and Mick stay with me.'

'I couldn't agree more.'

'You'll put it in writing?' she parried.

His lips thinned at that one.

'Come on, Dan, you're not short of a lawyer or three to whip something up for you.'

He exhaled, and shoved his hands deep into his designer

pockets. 'I'm disappointed you think you had to ask, Ava. I swear I've tried to make this a good deal for you. It's happening; you might as well just…' He waved frustrated hands.

'Lie back and think of England?'

A phone rang in an office somewhere. His mouth set dangerously. 'Thirteen episodes, Ava. That's it.'

And then she saw it: the tiniest glimmer of the younger man she remembered. Deep in those brown eyes was some fear that she'd take her skills and walk out. This *mattered* to him. That was her undoing. Instantly she was sixteen again, and every protective urge she'd spent years exorcising came bubbling to the surface. It galled her that she was still biologically opposed to hurting him.

'You hold my self-respect in your hands,' she said quietly. 'My career.'

He sighed and held her gaze. 'I know.'

'Give me your word it will be handled tastefully.' *That I will be.*

'You have it.' He stretched out a large hand. 'On your mother's memory.'

Ava glanced at his long fingers, at the tanned hand where it emerged from an expensive cuff. She itched to feel that smooth skin. But she forced herself to remember which side of the battlefield he'd chosen just minutes before. She stood straighter.

'If you had the slightest respect for my mother's memory you wouldn't be screwing her daughter over to further your own career.'

Even after nine years she still had enough residual hurt left in her to be satisfied as the colour leached entirely from Dan's face. Then she turned and walked from his office. It would be too easy to fall back on old times and trust him. She had to remember he was no longer Steve's best mate and her *de facto* big brother.

He was one of *them*.

The enemy.

CHAPTER TWO

'YOU are kidding, right?' Ava looked at her brother in confusion. 'I can't afford this!'

A magnificent home spread out before her, the deep blue of Sydney Harbour reflecting in its many tinted windows. It was sensational. Shooting six days a week for *Urban Nature* meant the ninety-minute commute to her south coast home just wasn't doable. Steve had warned her that city accommodation wouldn't come cheap, but even so she hadn't appreciated how much of her lucrative pay-rise would be eaten away.

He'd offered to scout affordable rentals for her in the week it would take her to pack up her life in Flynn's Beach. They'd looked at three already, but this opulence was by far his most ludicrous suggestion.

'You don't get it all.' Steven Lange took her shoulders and twisted her gently to face the east side of the residence. 'You get that bit.'

'What bit?'

'This bit.' A smooth voice cut in from her right, and Dan walked towards them, a newly cut key dangling from his fingers. She met his gaze evenly, almost defiantly, hoping he'd never realise she harboured the slightest remorse for the way she'd last spoken to him.

He clapped his hand on her brother's shoulder. 'Hey, mate. Good to see you.'

Steve grinned. 'Danno.'

A bad feeling came over her. *Oh, he hadn't...*

'Come on, I'll show you around my humble abode,' Dan said.

She turned and glared at Steve as Dan guided the way to a refurbished arched gate in the large rammed-earth wall that obscured the rest of the house from view. Ava's heart leapt as she stepped through the pretty gate into a small garden space, and her designer's eye immediately started doing its thing. There wasn't a lot of planning evident, but it was lush, flowering and completely unexpected in a house as modern as this one. An ancient birdbath leaned skew-whiff in the garden's heart. It was designer crooked, dotted with clusters of moss, and looked as if it belonged in a home magazine.

She fought to keep her face from betraying how much the whole setting appealed to her. It was precisely the sort of thing she might design.

'Garden and price, you said.' Steve spoke from behind her. 'They were your criteria. This has a garden, and you can afford it.'

Looking at the affluent surroundings, and considering it was in one of Sydney's top harbourside addresses, Ava struggled to imagine how she possibly could.

She lifted her chin and stared both men down. 'It also smacks of a set-up.'

Steve glanced away, but Dan wordlessly led them along a path made of rough-cut stone pavers and into a small guesthouse, which shared one wall with the main building. His tour of the little house ended in an airy bedroom, where he parted timber bi-fold doors and sunshine and fragrance from the garden spilled across the timber floor. Ava caught her breath and had to drag her focus back to her brother before she gave away how beautiful she found it.

Such a shame she wouldn't get to enjoy it.

Steve flopped onto the sofa in the living area. The throw draped so casually across it looked as if it was worth more than her entire budget lounge suite at home. Dan's new life certainly was a comfortable one.

'There must be other places on the list?' she said hopefully.

'Nup. Not with ticks in both boxes. And this one's close to the city and the waterfront as a bonus. You're not going to see better.'

She didn't doubt that for a second. The wash of the harbour was a tranquil soundtrack with the doors wide open like this, and it was just a ferry ride to the central business district. Lord, it was going to be hard to walk away from this one.

She turned to her brother. 'Come on, Steve, show me the list.'

His hands rose in a *mea culpa*. Dan spoke from behind her. 'Ava, take it. Just pretend you're living next to someone else.'

'It's not...' Lord, how did she begin to explain how she was feeling about all this now it was a reality? Working with him. Sharing a roof with him. *Him*. While she still felt so exploited.

'You're getting mates' rates,' Steve helpfully piped up.

She glared at him. That was a dirty pitch. He knew very well that finances were her Achilles' heel right now. 'How much?'

Steve looked to Dan for the answer, which meant Ava couldn't avoid it any longer. She dragged her eyes to his. He shrugged and said, 'It's part of your employment package.'

Free? This magnificent light and that gorgeous garden and harbour view were gratis? She forced the excitement down deep, visualised the revised contract she'd only just signed and looked Dan in the eye. 'No, it isn't.'

The tiniest hint of colour crept above the collar of his shirt. 'It's sitting here empty, Ava, and I'm hardly ever home. It's no skin off my nose if someone's living here.'

'What if you want to have guests to stay?' she asked.

He clamped his jaw hard. 'It won't be a problem.'

Because he had no friends? Or because most were of the female variety and would share his bedroom rather than the visitor's quarters? That nasty jealous whisper took her by surprise, and she twisted away to cross into the bedroom. Pettiness wasn't like her.

She looked again at the blossoming garden and imagined how it could look with a bit of time and focus. Then she thought about the many ways that her salary could be better spent than lining a stranger's pocket as rent. Just like that, a zero fell off her debt to the bank.

She glanced between Steve's hopeful grey eyes and Dan's veiled brown ones and chewed her lip. Which made her the bigger fool? Taking the guesthouse or knocking it back?

'Does it have its own entrance?' she hedged, desperate to find a valid fault.

'It's completely self-contained. And—' Dan guided her through the suite and out of the rear door, where a Winnebago barely fitted into the carport '—it comes with a mobile office. As agreed.'

Ava stepped past his guarded look and into the twenty-foot vehicle, with Steve following close behind. Her heart missed a beat.

'Courtesy of AusOne, for as long as you're with us,' Dan said. 'You can take this on location and work on your designs between shoots.'

It was ideal. Fully converted as an office space, with a drafting table, desk, filing cabinets and a kitchenette. Every inch of it was modern luxury, and no bigger than the horse-trucks she'd driven without problem for her dad. She was fast running out of good reasons to say no.

She clamped her jaw. 'Wow. When you guys sweeten, you really sweeten.'

'The network was…appreciative…of your situation, and eager to ensure you could work on location,' he said.

She shot him a wry glance. 'A happy host is a good host?'

He smiled, not quite relaxed, but it was the first she'd had from him since she'd seen him a week ago. The smile before that one had been more than nine years ago, before *that* night. She pushed the unwelcome thought from her head.

'You're not the host, truth be told,' he said.

'No?' Steve and Ava spoke together.

'You're the brains of the outfit. Brant Maddox is the anchor.'

'Ugh. Maddox.' Steve stomped out of the trailer in disgust. Ava frowned. Where had she heard that name before?

Dan clarified. 'Maddox is AusOne's latest and greatest.'

Oh, *right*! She grinned as she remembered. Brant Maddox was serious eye-candy. 'That should get you the female half of Australia watching, anyway.'

Dan held her look. 'You'll do all right with the male half, Ava. You forget, I've seen the test rushes.'

With no clue what to do with a compliment from Dan Arnot, Ava escaped the modern trailer office and returned into the world's most perfect guesthouse. Finding an affordable short-term rental in inner-Sydney wouldn't be easy for the six months she'd be here. This was pure luxury, central, a bargain, and she knew the landlord. All major plusses. And, of course, there was the magnificent light and the garden. She chewed her lip and looked everywhere but at the man standing next to her.

Could she do the girl-next-door thing again...?

Dan watched the conflict play out on Ava's face and tempered a smile. When she was young she'd used to have out-oud conversations with those voices in her head. Now it looked as if she'd mastered the art of internalisation.

Somewhat.

She'd walked away from him just now with as much dignity as when she'd marched from his office a week ago. Head high, as if she owned the place. Right now she wanted to. He could tell. The way her eyes had lit up when she saw the light streaming in the bedroom, and when she'd walked through the tiny garden courtyard.

But that light dimmed every time she looked at *him*. Like polished silver instantly aging.

He sighed and carefully closed the door to the trailer behind him, conscious of its price tag. If this season didn't go well, the leased RV and everything in it would be heading back to the dealers.

Bloody AusOne. He'd brought them a string of winners in his six years there, but one little sleeper in a glutted lifestyle market and suddenly they were *sending the boys round*. That meant forty jobs on the line—one of them Ava's.

Another one his. And he hadn't sacrificed a third of his life to give it all away this easily.

He leaned casually on the doorframe to the bedroom, dropped his voice and brought out the big guns. *He knew this woman*. At least the girl before the woman. Her habits couldn't have changed that much.

'Come on, Ava. Just imagine yourself stretched out in here having lazy Sunday afternoon naps, falling asleep to the sounds of the harbour.'

And just like that he had her. The grey eyes she turned on him brimmed with longing. Then, out of nowhere, his gut tightened, and he got a flash of long afternoons in there with her. But it was a different breed of longing in her eyes, and neither of them were napping.

He blinked the vision clear.

Watching her in the soft glow from outside reminded him of her test shots: how the light had seemed to radiate out from her rather than reflecting off her. She'd been on screen for less than five minutes of the behind-the-scenes special, but the test audience had rated her through the roof, responding unanimously to her vitality, her gentle nature and her absolute love of what she did. And it didn't hurt that she had a natural, earthy sexiness that any viewer with a Y-chromosome would respond to.

Dan certainly had. Lucky he was known for complete absorption during previews, or his total captivation might have been noticed. Little Ava was a now a certified knockout. Who would've thought it?

The last time he'd seen her she'd been all legs and teenage angst. A good kid, with a heart as big as a continent, right on the edge of womanhood, but high-maintenance in the extreme. And definitely not comfortable around him. That much, at least, hadn't changed.

'Excuse me.' Grown-up Ava avoided his eyes as she moved to pass him in the doorway.

He almost—almost—made her squeeze past him, but nine years had cured him of viewing her blushes as sport. He straightened and let her through, ignoring the subtle soapy scent that tantalised his senses and focussing on the challenge at hand.

He *needed* Ava on this show.

Urban Nature was practically made for her designs. Her talent for turning heavily urban spaces into green ones was as unique as it was inspired. Her proud brother had all too willingly fed Dan's need to vicariously monitor her progress and every design he delivered convinced Dan more and more that she was the key to a new concept in lifestyle. He'd offered her the designer's role on the pilot version of *Urban Nature* through a go-between, knowing she'd never willingly accept a job from him. Then, once she was well and truly hooked, he'd left it to Steve to break the bad news.

That she was really working for Daniel Arnot, scourge of Flynn's Beach…breaker of hearts.

Destroyer of dreams.

She locked eyes with him from across the suite and then glanced at the door leading to his part of the house. At the spanking new deadlock he'd installed yesterday. She looked somewhat comforted by it.

Dan forced down the regret and guilt at manipulating someone he considered a friend, a mate's sister. He'd worked too hard and sacrificed too much to retreat now. He had a point to prove to his old man and, by God, he was going to sharpen that point until it glinted.

The anticipation pulsing in his chest was all about his career goal suddenly being a heck of a lot closer. It had nothing to do with the woman looking back and forth between him and her brother.

So when she thrust out her hand and said, 'Okay. I'll take it,' the rush he felt could only have been the thrill of victory. Couldn't it?

CHAPTER THREE

'WHAT the..?'

Dan lengthened his strides as he approached the production trailer parked at the rear of the industrial property where they were shooting. More than one crew member had turned his head in the direction of two frazzled female voices—one raised and indignant, the other softer, more urgent. He climbed onto the trailer step with only a cursory knock and flung the door open.

On the periphery of his vision he saw the warning gaze of Carrie Watson, their make-up guru, but his attention was entirely consumed by five foot four inches of Ava.

Very angry Ava.

'Is this your idea?' she blazed, straight at him.

She stood, hands on hips, clad only in low-slung cargo shorts, which revealed a mile of tanned leg, and a brief—make that a *minuscule*—tank top. It was small, white, and disturbingly tight, with a logo for a popular brand of power tool stretched across her full chest. Every curve—and Ava had definitely been standing at the front of the queue when those were being dished out—screamed *notice me*.

'I'm digging a garden, Dan. Not dancing on a bar.'

He forced his eyes away from that logo. The last time he'd seen Ava in anything less than corporate wear she'd been sixteen years old. And this was definitely less. Way less. He sucked in some air.

'I'm not wearing it.' She stood legs apart, ready for a fight. A blistering one, by the looks of her.

His attention snapped back to her face as cold fury seeped in. This was not the outfit he'd signed-off on. No, this had network written all over it. It was only the first day of filming and Bill Kurtz was already playing games. He bustled past her to rummage in the small clothing rack in the corner.

'I couldn't agree more,' he said, reaching to pull a crisp pale blue shirt from its hanger.

'That's Brant's shirt,' Carrie hastily warned him. 'We need it for the next set-up.'

Dan fumed and shoved it back on the rack, glancing at Ava's clothes draped over the chair. She couldn't wear her own blouse; it was too busy for television. But she couldn't wear that…outift…either. It was completely the wrong image for the show.

Besides, he'd given her his word, and that get-up protected no one's integrity. Least of all his. He prowled around the trailer, looking for inspiration.

'They're going to want that logo in there, Dan,' Carrie reminded him unnecessarily.

'I know, Carrie. Just let me think.' Frustration made him short. They were filming in an industrial area, twenty minutes from the nearest shopping mall. That was a one-hour round trip the schedule just couldn't afford. The cursed network would know that.

He swore again.

His gaze landed on a blue singlet that sat unopened in its packet. On Ava it would be no better than her tank top, but it gave him an idea. He tugged his Yves Saint Laurent business shirt out of his waistband and made quick work of the dozen buttons.

'Here.' He thrust the still-warm shirt at Ava. 'Put this on over the top.'

It was too large by far, but she slid it on, and Carrie fashioned the excess fabric into a knot at her waist. The sponsor logo was still easily visible, but the result was infinitely less gratuitous.

Dan did his best not to look too closely. 'The shorts have to go, too,' he said. Exactly how Kurtz imagined those would work when Ava was digging in a garden bed in several shots… Oh, he knew exactly what Kurtz had imagined.

'I have cargo pants for tomorrow, Dan,' Carrie said, reaching to a low shelf.

'Perfect. Wear those,' he barked at Ava, then turned and nailed Carrie with his glare. 'Burn the shorts.'

He yanked the blue singlet from its packet and stalked out of the wardrobe trailer, tugging it on. He knew he'd snapped at both of them, but he was still reeling from his reaction to the skin-tight tank top. That chest. Those legs.

She was practically his little sister, for crying out loud.

He tucked the singlet in, not caring how ridiculous it looked over suit pants. It wasn't a patch on how ridiculous Ava would have looked in the get-up the network had switched to. Thank God he'd been on set today.

He was going to have to watch the filming like a hawk.

'Wow!' Carrie unfroze just long enough to snap her gaping mouth closed. She blinked in the direction that Cyclone Dan had just blown through.

The image of that sculpted chest free of its expensive covering burned into Ava's brain like a cheap plasma television. Last time she'd seen it, it had been slick with sweat and barrelling towards her in the dark of night. She swallowed the thought and turned away from the doorway as the warmth of Dan's shirt soaked into her. She met Carrie's eyes for a moment, and they burst out laughing.

'I'm sorry I was being a princess about the tank top,' Ava said. Prima donna was no way to start a working relationship.

'Oh, love—forget it. I wouldn't have worn it either. I'm just amazed you got away with it. He's a *producer*, you know.' Carrie shook her head and went back to placing out the tiny pots and brushes that were the tools of her trade.

Ava had already discovered that the higher up the food chain you got in television the less popular you became, but she felt obliged to defend Dan. For old times' sake if nothing else.

'He's all right.'

'Honey, for what he just did the man's a hero. You know he's going to take some flak for that. I wouldn't like to be a fly on the wall when the network sees the dailies from this shoot.'

Ava ran her hand along the smooth collar of the business shirt and turned partly away from Carrie to breathe her fill of Dan's distinctive cologne. The rich scent mingled with his own personal smell. How many years had she been as sensitive as a tracker dog to that particular scent? Until she'd exorcised it through necessity.

The fabric was warm, fragrant, and hideously expensive—and she was about to start shovelling dirt with it on. The irony made her smile.

Carrie steered her to the well-used chair in front of the trailer's mirror. 'Sit yourself down, love. If Dan's butt is on the line, let's give it some company.'

Twenty minutes later Ava stared at her reflection. She knew she had a face full of make-up, but Carrie had applied it so subtly it looked as if she was wearing virtually none. Enormous grey eyes stared at her from the mirror, artfully highlighted with kohl, her skin was wrinkle-free—for that alone Carrie deserved a medal—and her honey-blonde hair was restrained in a tight ponytail that managed to accentuate the long curve of her neck while still looking completely effortless. She'd never been one to overplay her strengths. She had a good mind and a good heart and those assets meant the most to her. But for the first time ever Ava looked at her own face and didn't count her flaws.

Her heart lifted slightly.

Minutes later she stepped out of the trailer, shrouded in Dan's shirt and wearing the practical cargos. She tossed the shortie-shorts in the trash on the way out and farewelled Carrie.

An ally. Exactly what she needed on a day like today. She could do with a friend on set.

You have one, a tiny voice reminded her. A friend of many years.

But Dan had chosen the other side in this whole mess. Despite the chivalry of this morning, he was still corporate with a capital 'C'. Still the boss. Inevitably the time would come when he would remind her of that fact, and any shred of friendship they had left would be nothing but history.

It was daunting to be the centre of attention, taking commands from a swag of people with their own jobs to do, trying to follow various instructions while remembering what she was supposed to be there for.

Read this. Say that. Step here and you'll be off camera. Step there and you'll be out of the light.

Her patience was just about shot by the time Dan reappeared on set, his suit jacket slung over the blue singlet. He moved so comfortably through the throng it was easy to see why he was successful at what he did. He still oozed confidence. So much so he made pairing a workman's singlet with suit pants seem almost normal.

Ava glanced away, not wanting to stare.

Slightly behind Dan came a vision she couldn't help but appreciate. His Hollywood smile lit a path straight towards her and she blinked as he turned its full force onto her.

Brant Maddox. Host and celebrity hottie.

'Ava. Such a pleasure to meet you.' Brant's hand closed around hers. Warm, smooth...but empty. Nothing like the sure grip of the darker man beside him. She frowned at the comparison. Before she could return the greeting, Brant's hand tugged her in to kiss her cheek. She stumbled and fell into him, still conscious that the tank top magnified her assets.

Brant seemed pleased with the heat flaming in her cheeks and stepped away. An odd expression flitted across his blue eyes. *My work here is done*, they seemed to say. Had the whole encounter been manufactured for effect? What was his story?

'Ava Lange—Brant Maddox.' Dan's belated introductions were pointless, but Ava appreciated his businesslike tone. It helped her remember why she was there.

'Ava, can I have a word?' He held up five fingers to the director, who then called a break to the crew. She followed him off to one side, smiling an unnoticed farewell at Brant, who was now thoroughly engaged in chatting to his next target. Dan steered her with a gentle hand to her back. Heat soaked through his shirt to her skin where he touched her.

Down, girl...

'You look great,' he said, examining her dispassionately. 'Much better.'

Offence nipped in her belly and her eyebrows rose. 'They don't call them artists for nothing.'

He looked at her more closely then. 'I was talking about the clothes. But now you mention it, yes, she's done a great job with your make-up. Natural.' He scrutinised the whole picture again, trailing his eyes over her face slowly and thoroughly.

Two blushes in two minutes. Even for her that was something. She glanced at the set, uncomfortable with his intense regard.

He cleared his throat, back to business. 'Two things. Your latest design is brilliant—possibly your best yet.'

The glow that warmed her body irked her. She shouldn't need his endorsement to feel proud about this design. She'd channelled all her frustration and anger at being coerced by the network into the most beautiful garden she could create. It had resulted in some of her best work.

'Thank you. I figured that if it's my face, now, as well as my name on it, then I'd better make it a knockout.'

His chocolate eyes studied her closely. They did nothing to ease the warmth in her cheeks.

'You've succeeded,' he said. 'Although I had to lean on our suppliers for better prices to afford some of the centrepieces.'

She smiled sweetly. A pair of massive ornamental *dracaenas* would have added a zero to the budget all by their spiky selves. It felt magnificent to finally get one over on Mr Smugness himself.

Almost too good. Addictive. Her body stirred.

'I'm just looking for an indication as to whether you're planning on maintaining that level of terrorism by design,' he said.

Her laugh tinkled even to her own ears. 'I can give you no guarantees.'

'Just remember it's not the network whose day you're making harder with those little rebellions.'

She smiled and held his gaze. Pure innocence. 'No?'

He smiled, too. A sexy, knowing kind of smile. 'No. And not mine either, although I'm sure that was your intent.' He steered her further away from prying ears. The heat radiating from where his hand closed over her elbow was both comforting and disturbing. 'Tania from Procurement spent a whole day trying to get you what you wanted within the budget she'd been set. She was embarrassed to have to tell me she couldn't do it.'

Ava's smile instantly dropped. 'Oh. Not my intention.' Talk about backfire!

'I know. I just wanted to point it out.'

How could he know her so well even after nine years apart? He had the uncanny knack of reaching right into her mind and plucking her thoughts like daisies.

'Okay. Lesson learned,' she said. 'What was the second thing?'

He assessed her for a moment before continuing. 'Brant Maddox.'

Ava's eyes found Brant in the jumble of crew, casually leaning on an upturned urn, chatting to an assistant—although there was really nothing casual about it. Again, he was posing for anyone paying attention. A picture of casual male beauty.

'Speaking of expensive ornamentals…'

Dan laughed quietly and looked at her through those killer lashes. 'Okay, so maybe I don't need to worry about point number two.'

Realisation struck. 'Oh, you were *not*…' He was going to warn her about Maddox? 'You, of all people!'

It was Dan's turn to flush—just slightly, but with no corporate collar to hide it she saw colour steal its way up his tanned throat.

'I'm thinking about the show, Ava. We can't afford any interpersonal issues that might screw things. There's too much riding on this.'

She straightened, armed and dangerous. 'And of course you automatically assume I would be the screw-up. That I wouldn't have the same appreciation of the importance of this.'

'You said it yourself, Ava. You don't value it.'

'No, but *you* do.' Her raised voice drew a few curious glances from the crew. She dropped it carefully and let her eyes burn into his. 'I wouldn't do that to you, Dan.'

Despite everything he'd done—now and nine years ago—that was true. She had no interest in causing him harm. But…it didn't hurt to remind him that he hadn't been as considerate of *her* needs.

'That's generous of you, under the circumstances…'

It was the first time she'd seen him look uncomfortable. Just when she'd thought he wasn't capable of it. 'I'm a generous woman, Dan.'

Her flippant reply took on a whole new meaning as his eyes flickered to the logo on her shirt. It was such a brief moment she thought she might have imagined it, but her skin tingled all over at the suspicion.

He spoke quietly. 'Thank you, Ava. That's more than I deserve.'

Oh. The man certainly knew how to throw her off kilter. All the fight drained out of her. She cleared her throat. 'Shall we get to work?'

Dan stepped away so Ava could return to the middle of the ugly concrete rooftop where they had three days to transform it into a world-class rooftop garden. She looked completely in her element, and surprisingly at ease with the attention now centred on her. Attention she'd been loath to accept.

The Ava he remembered from childhood had always been

gutsy, a rampant tomboy, until one day around her thirteenth birthday a switch had flipped and she'd suddenly discovered she was female. She'd been ragingly shy from then on, the only female left in an all-male family after her mother died when she was eight. The baby by four years, too, which meant she'd been frequently over-protected.

Looking at her now, smiling up at something inane Maddox was saying, professional respect warred deep in Dan's gut with the blinding desire to protect her. He frowned as the feeling shifted south.

Or was it just plain desire?

She was hardly little Ava now. Grown. Talented. Attractive. Beautiful in this moment, with the television lights shining down on her. But she was still Steve's little sister. Virtually his, too.

But not quite.

Not that he wouldn't have killed to be part of their family for real.

Maddox looked at her and spoke, hitting her with one of those perfect smiles that Dan had seen work so often on women in the network. She tipped her head and laughed. The sound danced right over to where he stood watching, and the urge to protect surged in him again.

Steve's kid sister. He had responsibilities here. Professionally and personally.

He'd have to stay on his toes.

CHAPTER FOUR

THE voices were back. Whispering. Urgent.

Even through the thick veil of sleep Ava knew that couldn't be good. Not again…

No one ever whispered in the Lange household. They did everything at mega decibels. But what were the chances, on the eve of her sixteenth birthday, that secrecy and whispers could mean anything other than a surprise being hatched? She shook the beach sand from her hair and tiptoed, smiling, to the kitchen, then crouched, frozen, by the doorway.

It was Dan. Three years of undivided attention had a way of branding a voice into your brain. And that must be her brother with him but—really—who cared? Gorgeous, talented, spectacular Dan was conjuring up a birthday surprise.

For her.

Did anyone else matter? Her heart kicked up three notches.

'Ava's not twelve any more,' Steve's voice whispered, deeper than usual.

Dan sighed before he answered. 'Believe me, I know.'

Ava frowned. His sad voice didn't make him sound as if he was plotting anything fun. Her skin prickled.

'You should say something—'

'I can't,' Dan said. 'When she turns those beautiful eyes on me…how can I?'

Her heart beat like the wings of a honeyeater. Dan was

talking about her! He thought her eyes were beautiful. After so many years of seeing her as a kid, he'd finally noticed she was a woman. Nearly.

Tomorrow.

Ava's legs thrashed painfully amongst her bedclothes as the dream images morphed into a Flynn's Beach backyard, minutes away from midnight.

The lights were off in Dan's converted games room, but that didn't slow Ava down. She'd chosen her best skirt and blouse—strategically short-buttoned—and practised her speech in the mirror fifty times, so she'd know exactly how to stand when delivering it and exactly how she'd look as she did.

Her empty stomach trembled. Dan wouldn't be able to help but take her in his arms and kiss her until they were both breathless.

She'd practised that too. Over and over while sequestered away for three years, pining for a young man who was, miraculously and unexpectedly—going to be hers.

God, would she even know what to do with him? An unfamiliar tightness and an unbearable excitement overcame her.

She was practically part of the furniture in Dan's retreat, so turning the unlocked handle without knocking seemed a perfectly reasonable thing to do…at midnight…in the dark…

The door swung inwards and she whispered his name into the darkness…

Ava forced her eyes open on an outraged shout. Her pulse galloped beneath sweat-dampened skin and she lurched up onto her elbows to force air into desperate, aching lungs.

At least this time she'd woken herself before the worst part.

Before the congealed, nine-year-old montage accented by moonlight: the illicit sheen of Dan's toned buttocks; the long length of female leg bent skywards; the sweat-slicked contours of a grown man's chest as he twisted towards where Ava stood, horrified, in the doorway.

Her own agonised sprint down to the beach with Dan's angry oath echoing in her ears.

Ava's body shuddered with mini-convulsions. *Why?* She'd been dream-free for a year. A whole blessed year. She'd thought the nights of thrashing and trembling were finally behind her. It had been bad enough living through it the first time, without reliving it over and again courtesy of her subconscious.

Damn him.

She swung her legs out from under the twisted wreckage of her bedcovers and slowly put her weight on both feet. It wouldn't be the first time her legs had failed her after the dream, but tonight they held. She pushed upright and picked her way carefully to the guesthouse kitchenette.

Coffee. Now.

Too bad it was only two a.m. There was no chance in Hades that Ava was going to let herself fall back to sleep. Not tonight. Not if it meant going back to the agony of her memories.

She set the kettle to rapid boil.

It didn't take a psych major to work out why the dream had returned. She hadn't counted on working this closely with Dan; hadn't expected him to be so hands-on. It made keeping some distance between them challenging and keeping the memories at bay impossible. They retreated away from shore by day, but surged back like a moontide at night.

She rubbed her closed eyes.

The first sip of coffee helped to settle her churning stomach. The second slowed her trembles. It was hot and strong and so terribly normal it chased some of the demons away. But not all of them. The little guesthouse suddenly felt claustrophobic.

Tiny and crowded and…Dan's.

The man sleeping just metres away. The man who had chased after her that night, still buttoning the denim glued to him like a second skin. Still with an acre of bare chest. Still smelling of a strange woman and sex.

Ava surrendered to the urgent desire to be far away. She let herself out through the bedroom doors and tiptoed with her coffee through the garden, beyond the rammed-earth archway to the water's edge. Harbourview Terrace at two a.m. wasn't too far removed from Flynn's Beach at midnight. Quiet, tranquil, private.

She self-medicated again with a gulp of hot caffeine.

Sixteen. Such a blind age. And so horribly, horribly fragile. There'd been a moment back then—hidden away in her favourite grotto on the beach—where she'd thought she might be able to come up with a credible reason for having appeared at his door at midnight. But the complete fatal understanding in his eyes when he'd found her there had robbed her of that hope.

He'd tried to be gentle with her, but she'd shrugged him off violently, tears fuelled by excruciating humiliation racking her body.

Every time she had the dream, every time the carnal montage played back in her unprotected subconscious, she relived the mortification as though it were fresh. Her heart tightened until it hurt. From her spot by the water the lights of Sydney were a blurry, incandescent mush through eyes awash with remembered pain.

Sixteen.

For a girl with not a lot of life experience she'd certainly had a finely honed instinct for what would hurt. Demanding to know—as if she'd had any right at all—who the woman in his room was. Knowing before he'd even answered that she was a surfer. The woman's blonde hair, tanned, toned muscles and enormous cartoon breasts had been a dead giveaway.

She remembered crossing her arms protectively over her own pathetic efforts and letting nasty Ava out to play. It had felt good. Given the pain somewhere to go.

'How does she stay upright on the surfboard?' she'd sneered.

The censure in the way he'd clipped her name then had hurt almost as much as seeing him lying on top of someone else. Hearing the hoarse ecstasy in his groan.

'I'm twenty years old, Ava. I can sleep with whomever I like.'

Just not me, Ava thought now—not for the first time. Dan had never seen her as anything other than a child.

But his eyes when she'd angered him that night... They'd flooded with the same passion she'd glimpsed in them in the nanosecond before she'd fled out of his bedroom, and for the first time in her life her teenaged body had responded sensually.

Like a woman.

Ava drained the last of her coffee, shifting on the limestone levy to dislodge the uncomfortable tightening of her nipples that plagued her even now. Back then the feeling had confused her, surprised her.

But nowhere near as much as it had surprised Dan.

She remembered his exact expression as the tightening had drawn his focus to the buttons still undone on her blouse. Confused fire had flashed in those molten depths and he'd ripped his eyes violently away from the lace-covered curve of her young breasts. Breasts that had suddenly been aching.

His eyes had widened. The horror on his face had spoken volumes. It had made Ava's breath catch as she'd fumbled the blouse buttons into their eyelets.

'We're just friends, Ava.'

Lord, that had been like steel wool on sunburn. He didn't love her. Or even want her. Her heart had sunk beneath an ocean of shame. She'd wanted to run out into the dark ocean, make a miserable meal for some shark. But something imperceptible and irrevocable had shifted in the moment that her body had responded to the fire in his.

She'd grown up.

She held her breath now, remembering how close his half-naked body had suddenly felt in her beach grotto, how the frost of her breath in the cold night air had mingled with his. How he'd been both the cause and the only analgesic for the throbbing pain in her heart.

Her lips had fallen open and she'd locked eyes with him. Absolutely nothing on this earth to lose. One hundred percent woman.

One hundred percent deluded.

The *doof-doof* of a heavy bass beat dragged her attention back to the small harbourside park between her and the guest-house. This might remind her of Flynn's Beach, but she'd do well to remember that it wasn't. This was Sydney. And that was a car full of young men out cruising after a night on the turps.

She let the car pass harmlessly by, then dragged herself to her feet and turned for the house. She'd been lost in her memories for over an hour out here. They swamped her, refusing to be set aside.

As she returned to the house, she noticed a light on at the back of Dan's side of the house. Awareness bristled on her nape. Why was he up at three a.m.? Was he walking off disturbing vivid dreams too? Was he thinking about that night on the beach? How they'd fought?

The realist in her slapped those thoughts down. He was probably not even alone. A man like Dan was hardly likely to be wandering the halls pining for a woman like her. *Particularly* not her.

He'd been more than clear that night on the beach. He'd recognised her unspoken invitation, had stared at her for eternal moments, and then dragged his focus away—out to sea. When he'd brought it back, his eyes had been hard and empty.

Ava hadn't seen them like that since he'd first come to her family, years before. His lips had paled, his jaw had tightened, and then he'd uttered the words that had burned into her young soul for ever.

'I'll never be with you, Ava—'

She'd failed miserably to disguise her flinch at the cruelty in those words. It had been like being dumped by the biggest, coldest wave conceivable. Air-stealing, baffling, aching pain. She'd scrambled to right herself on the ocean bottom.

'You're a child; I'm a grown man—'

Had he thought she wouldn't understand the cold finality of those words? Had he truly needed to grind salt straight into the gaping wound in her chest? It burned again now, a referred pain from years ago. She'd never been enough for him.

'—with the interests and needs of a grown man. Neither of which you could help much with, kiddo.'

Ava stiffened against what had come next. Her blinding attack. The indiscriminate slashing of a mortally wounded young woman. Anything to hurt him the way she'd been hurting. She closed her eyes. Oh, the poison that had poured from her lips... She'd attacked his intelligence, his integrity, and—she shook her head—his surfing. His only love in the world. By the time she was done, his hands had been shaking.

'I was wrong to think we could get past this.' He'd moved to stand. 'I'm leaving in the morning—'

And just when she'd thought she had no heart left to break, she'd felt it rip completely free of her chest. He was leaving. On her birthday. The terror of losing him had cracked headlong against the hurt of his rejection, giving birth to a bright spark that had ignited the rocket-fuel of anger in her belly.

She'd never again spoken to another human being the way she'd spoken to him then. Shouting, crying. Dying.

'You *should* leave. You've been like a blowfly hanging around ever since I can remember. Go find your own family!'

Stupid with grief, she'd shot to her feet and pursued him when he'd stalked off, unable to stomach the sight of her.

'Like mother like son, huh, Dan? Running off when the going gets tough.'

The kettle's song interrupted the painful memory, and Ava realised that it was tears, not steam, which dampened the kitchen benchtop. Her heart pounded with the realism of the ancient memory, and her throat ached as if she was still sixteen. She recalled vividly the anger in his eyes as he'd spun around and surged back towards her. She'd never in her life seen him so...dark. She had stumbled backwards, but his words had hit her like a barrage of gunfire.

'I will *never* be with you, Ava. I don't know how to make myself any clearer. I'm sorry if that hurts you, but you need to understand.'

Then he'd turned and stalked out of the grotto. And out of her life.

When she'd woken to her father's gentle touch and his sombre, 'Happy sweet sixteenth, princess,' she'd known he'd already gone.

After the humiliation and agony of that night she'd never let someone get close again. She'd lost her confidence, her dignity. Her friend. She'd trussed up her heart in a lead box and buried it in the deepest abyss of her consciousness. She channelled herself into her schoolwork, then her studies, then her employment, and finally her business.

Daniel Arnot had taught her how to be impenetrable. It was a successful strategy that had achieved its goal perfectly.

Until now.

Now her protective casing had been peeled back, leaving her exposed and vulnerable to the one man who had hurt her more than any other. Not that he'd shown the slightest interest in her other than as an asset to his company. A dollar sign on a profit and loss report.

And probably just as well, because—judging by her feelings tonight, by her body's physical response to events that had happened nearly a decade ago—if Daniel chose to turn all that Arnot charm on her she'd be powerless to prevent her body and her heart from overthrowing her carefully reinforced mind.

And that would be a very bad day.

Ava hugged her coffee close, stared at the brightening clouds of morning, and let a decade of pain stream down her face.

CHAPTER FIVE

DAN'S assistant let Ava into his spacious office and encouraged her to make herself comfortable. She moved towards the window, her arms wrapped protectively around her. She was still raw from her restless night, but more determined than ever, in the cold light of day, to find a way to exorcise Dan from her heart.

His office wasn't on the top floor, but it was close. And it was nearly bigger than the entire guesthouse in Harbourview Terrace. The last time she'd been here, she'd been too angry to really appreciate the tasteful decorations and magnificent outlook. She stared across the water. Somewhere on the other side was his sprawling waterfront house. Her temporary home.

He had certainly done well for himself in the years since he'd walked out on her family.

She'd kept up her awareness at first, through her brother, but after a while it had been easier not to ask. Not to wonder. It had just hurt too much to hear about his life. The many girlfriends. The great city career. She looked around. He must have worked hard to forge the sort of success that led to this kind of opulence at his relatively young age.

She trailed her fingers along the hardwood bookshelves, full of marketing and commerce tomes. She wondered if he read them or whether they were props. It didn't matter what he wore or how big his office was, Ava had a hard time imagining him as the executive type. She remembered him as a young man in love with the ocean, not with the stock market. He'd been all set to become a pro-surfer.

'We've come a long way, haven't we?'

She spun around, embarrassed to be caught browsing the contents of his shelves. Her eyes caught the large indoor ficus now standing where the bamboo had been a few weeks ago. 'What happened to your *phyllostachys*?'

'Antibiotics cleared it right up.' She blinked at him. He moved to his desk and flipped open a panel covered in buttons, smiling to himself. 'Kidding, Ava. I moved the bamboo out of here a few weeks ago for some time outdoors. I noticed you weren't happy with its condition.'

He had? Ava could barely remember looking at it. Her lips moved of their own will. 'The ficus will do better.'

She fell to silence, but it was a far cry from the comfortable silences they'd once shared. In the good old days. Before hormones.

He waved a disk. 'You did well these past two days. I've got some footage if you'd like to see it?'

Her stomach flipped. Oh, Lord—did she? Standing in front of a camera was one thing, but watching herself played back in close-up was quite another.

'What if I stink?'

He smiled and closed the office door, until only an inch of light streamed in from the outer office. 'You don't stink. Quite the opposite.'

She sank onto the sofa in front of the large screen while Dan loaded the disk. Automatic blinds slid out of nowhere across the window and the lights in the office dropped as the television hummed to life.

'These are only dailies, so they haven't been edited or balanced yet,' he warned.

On screen, Ava looked nervous, glancing around the rooftop set anxiously as the tape rolled before anyone called *action*. A sound assistant shot into frame briefly, to better disguise her radio microphone, and then she was alone on screen again. The camera zoomed right in on her eye, focussed sharp, and then pulled back out.

'You look terrified,' Dan commented through the darkness. 'But wait…'

Ava watched herself glance off to one side for the barest moment, see something there, and then turn her face back towards the camera. The fear and tension faded. She took a deep breath, tugged Dan's business shirt more securely across her front, and smiled.

Dan froze the image and that brilliant smile lit the office. She jumped as his voice sounded right behind her.

'What did you see? Then…when you looked away?'

Ava knew exactly. She remembered it. But no way was she going to tell him.

I saw you.

He'd walked past with the director and given her an encouraging smile just as she was about to start. At the time she'd appreciated the show of support, but had no clue what a difference it had made to her face, her fear. Until now. She looked at the giant eyes on screen and recognised that dazzled expression one hundred percent.

Oh, Ava, girl, you're going to have to learn to cover that up.

'I don't know,' she lied. 'There was a lot going on.'

'Well, whatever it was it was good. It put you in a different place. Watch how you change.' Dan thumbed the 'play' button and the first to-camera segment began. On-screen-Ava introduced herself and spoke briefly about the inner city roof space they'd be working on. She dropped a line mid-way through, paused, and calmly commenced again from that point, running smoothly through until Brant walked into the shot on cue.

She was no actress, but she wasn't bad either. Relief trickled through her body. Dan sank onto the sofa next to her as the disk played on. There was a second take of the whole introductory segment, and then some straight-to-camera pieces of Brant's.

Then there was a two-shot, with herself and Brant walking through the desolate urban roof space.

'You look good together,' Dan murmured from the shadows next to her ear.

'That's what Brant said.'

'Hmm...I'll bet.'

Ava smiled, distracted by the scene playing out. She was going to have to get used to seeing herself on screen. She understood suddenly why television starlets were so bird-like in reality. The camera forgave nothing. Well, they'd wanted 'healthy'...

The footage played through, and Ava smiled at the vaguely flirtatious on-camera interaction of her co-host. It made for good television, and it was nowhere near as sleazy on camera as it had felt in person. Brant obviously had a good instinct for what worked on screen.

When the entire disk had played, Dan lounged next to her, his arm slung across the sofa-back in the darkness. Without the monitor casting its sickly glow, the only illumination in the room was a thin shaft of light that spilled in from the outer office. Otherwise it was just the two of them, alone in the dark. Ava stiffened.

'What do you think?' He was disturbingly close. Ava forced herself to ignore the ambrosial scent of his aftershave. Like something mixed especially for her from her favourite things.

Ocean, forest and Dan.

She wasn't used to blowing her own trumpet, but she actually didn't stink! 'I'm happy with it. Are you?'

Dan made a so-so gesture and her heart sank. 'For a first day, yes, it's good,' he said. 'There are some things we need to tighten.'

What he thought shouldn't have mattered so much, but disappointment flooded through her at his less than enthusiastic response. 'It's only the first day...'

'It's also the first thing new viewers will watch. We sink or swim on that first day's shooting.'

He was right, but she struggled to see what was so terribly

wrong with it. Naturally, he enlightened her. 'The lighting wasn't even between shots,' he went on. 'Some of the camera work could have been tighter. Your movements weren't the height of grace…'

Ava's cheeks burned in the darkness. He'd have to feel the furnace cooking away next to him, surely? She put her hands up to dampen the heat as excuses started tumbling across her lips.

'It wasn't the same as the run-throughs. The layout of the rooftop was different in rehearsal…'

I've never done this before!

'We'll be rescheduling to allow rehearsals on location to help with that. So you'll feel more comfortable when we roll.'

Ava felt the bite of his censure—all too like that other time. Thank God for the low light. 'Was there anything you *were* happy with?'

'Sure. Your to-camera work is great. The sound was faultless. And the byplay between yourself and Maddox is fun. That'll sell.'

Ah, yes. Ratings. What would work well on television and what wouldn't. Presumably a clod-footed host stumbling over air-conditioning ducts wouldn't. Ava swallowed her pride and listened as Dan outlined the changes he wanted to make before the next shoot. If she could have separated her brain from her heart she would have recognised they were nothing dramatic or particularly difficult. Nothing that a second day of experience wouldn't fix.

But as she sat in the dark, listening to Dan's honey voice pulling her performance to pieces, she just couldn't be dispassionate about it. His opinion mattered. His disappointment hurt.

'Ava?'

'Sorry? What?'

Irritation tightened his tone. 'Was there anything you wanted to ask me? Anything you don't understand?'

I don't understand how you can have changed so much.

'No. I'm good.'

He shifted in the dark. Paused. 'I've upset you.'

The obtuseness in his voice was the absolute last straw. 'Why would you say that? Just because I did my very best, with no experience and not much instruction?' She surged to her feet. 'This was *your* plan, Dan, not mine. If I'm not quite what you were hoping for then you can talk it over with your network buddies and fire me. I'm all too happy to return to my design work and chalk this up as a really bad idea.' She stumbled to her feet.

'Ava, wait…' Dan's hand closed around hers as she yanked the door open. Light pooled in from the outer office, illuminating the regret in his face. She knew it must also show the hurt and anger in hers. He pulled her into the office—into him— letting the door swing closed again. The darkness was like a warm cloak around her.

'I'm sorry. I forgot you're new to the idea of critical feedback.'

Ava dropped her lashes, ashamed at her unprofessional outburst, but not ready to *still* not be good enough for him.

'I should have taken more care,' he said gently, his thumb stroking the underside of her wrist. It was strangely comforting. And more than a bit distracting. 'You've always been so tough, Ava. Scrabbling straight to your feet after wrecking your bike. Backing younger kids in a fight.'

He was gentling her now, making good on his mistake, but knowing that didn't change its effect on her one bit. She softened like butter in summer.

'I wanted to do well.' *For you.*

'You did do well, Ava. Did you expect to be perfect?'

She blushed. 'Yes. I hoped to be.'

'Ah. Revenge?'

He understood. She remembered that about him. He always got her. Her voice was wry. 'I was hoping to stick it to the faceless suits at the network by being the best I could possibly be.'

He pulled her close, away from any prying ears in the outer office, sure that at least one of them was supplementing their income courtesy of Bill Kurtz. 'Your logic is fuzzy at times, kiddo. You want to punish them by proving them right?'

'Don't call me that.' She stiffened. 'I'm not a kid any more.'

'No, you're not.' He kept her wrist in his velvet grip, and the husky tone in his voice had her glancing up at him in the half-darkness. 'I realised that the moment I walked into the wardrobe trailer yesterday.'

His thumb grazed over her pulse-point. She swallowed. Hard. 'I'm fine now, Dan. You can let go. Hissy fit is over.'

He didn't let go. 'What are you doing for dinner?'

The rapid change of subject had her reeling. That or the feel of his skin pressed so perfectly against hers. 'Uh…I hadn't thought about it. Something simple?'

'Want some company?'

The thought of eating in the guesthouse alone with Dan was too much to contemplate. 'I was thinking of trying one of the local cafés.'

'Aardvark is good.'

She couldn't help a laugh. 'The mammal or the venue?'

When he released her hand, Ava felt the loss keenly. 'It's a waterfront café. Excellent chilli mussels.'

Sheesh, was there a single button that Dan hadn't remembered? The idea of a whopping great bowl of her favourite mollusc dominated her mind the moment he planted it there.

'Okay.' Without even touching her, Dan held Ava in complete thrall. She was powerless to move. She stared at his handsome face and wondered what he was working up to say to her. It looked serious.

'Mr Arnot?' A voice interrupted from the outer office.

Dan tensed immediately, but didn't take his eyes from Ava's. 'Yes, Grace?'

'Mr Kurtz on line one. He says it's urgent.'

A moment went by before he peeled his gaze away and the lights suddenly brightened. Ava blinked. There was not a trace in his expression of the gentle coaxing of barely moments ago.

Had she completely imagined it? Wishful thinking?

He nudged her towards the door. 'After all, we both have to eat. Might as well do it together.' The words were impersonal. Convenient. All business.

I must have imagined it. She sucked in a baffled breath, then walked alone out of the room.

Dan swore and turned to his empty office. It wasn't often he felt comfortable in his own space, regardless of its splendour. Standing in the dark with Ava he'd felt as close to relaxed as he ever had here.

'Line one, Mr Arnot.' Grace called a reminder through to him. He snatched the phone and punched the blinking light with a brisk greeting.

'How did our new talent go this week?' Bill Kurtz wasted no time with niceties. His questions were usually loaded, and Dan knew the Executive Producer would have seen each day's footage before he had himself.

'Good,' he said. 'Great, in fact. A few tech issues, but nothing we can't iron out tomorrow.'

Kurtz snorted. 'Better than good, I'd say. She's a doll. And she's the perfect accessory for Maddox.'

'She's more than an accessory, Bill. She gives the show its street cred—'

'Course she does, course she does...'

Okay, so you're not looking for conversation. So what do you want?

Kurtz barrelled on. 'She wasn't really dressed the way we expected, though...'

Ah.

'But the whole farm girl thing worked for me,' Kurtz said. 'Fresh-faced. Innocent. That was a good call on your part.' Dan gnashed his teeth. 'The client will be happy, and if the client's happy...'

...Kurtz is happy. Dan knew it well. Just as he knew what happened if a client wasn't happy. He thought of Ava, waiting

for him downstairs, and how he'd bundled her so rudely out of his office. This was not a conversation he'd want her to over-hear. But Kurtz wasn't as livid as he'd been expecting. Which made him immediately suspicious.

'Was there something else, Bill?'

'Just one thing…'

Here we go…

'About Maddox. I like what's going on with them in the dailies. That spark. They work well together. I want you to exploit it, Dan.'

Dan's lips tightened; his tone cooled. 'In what way, Bill?'

'Hell, I don't know. Throw them together more. Give 'em more interplay. Sex it up a bit. You're paid to work that stuff out.'

Dan pinched the bridge of his nose and closed his eyes. 'Sex it up?'

'Audiences love chemistry, Dan. Will they? Won't they? The wondering…'

'We're a lifestyle show, Bill. Not daytime,' Dan said.

The phone almost frosted over in his hand. 'This is not a ne-gotiation, Dan. I want to see sparks flying between those two. You have a reputation as the go-to-guy for brave programming, so let's see a little courage here. Stretch the envelope. Prove that our faith in your choice of presenter was not misplaced.'

As if they hadn't forced his hand to consider using Ava like this in the first place… Dan's jaw ached. His dentist was going to be buying a new Mercedes if he didn't ease up on his enamels.

But he knew when to affect a strategic retreat. The harder Dan leaned, the harder Kurtz would lean. It was a case of pick your battles with the unpleasant senior executive. If it had been just him at risk he'd have leaned harder; it was in his nature. But with forty other employees and their jobs in the mix…forty-one if he counted Ava…he'd have to suck it up.

This time.

Ava and Maddox. His stomach turned over. 'I'll see what I can do, Bill. We'll need to introduce it slowly or audiences won't buy it. Don't expect a Royal Wedding.'

'Not for a moment,' came the insincere response. 'I just expect you to do the best thing by the network. I know how much it means to you.'

The older man rang off, leaving Dan glaring angrily into space. Kurtz knew exactly how important Dan's career was to him, how ruthlessly he'd worked over the past six years to make it to producer. A few more wins and he was on track to be the youngest executive producer Australian television had ever seen. What a handy tool to wave around in his face. To threaten him with.

Sex it up.

Dan grunted. There was no question Ava wouldn't tolerate it. Most likely she'd tell him and the network exactly where they could shove their sparks. He hadn't needed to grow up with her to know that. He tugged his suit jacket on over his Hugo Boss shirt. Immediately he flashed back to draping his shirt around Ava's bare shoulders, to her standing between his arms, afire. It was disturbingly vivid.

His body tightened.

He sighed. He'd seen exactly what Kurtz saw. There *was* a noticeable...something...between his two co-stars—a relaxed kind of ease. He tried to imagine how it might be to be on the receiving end of that ease and couldn't. Ava just wasn't comfortable around him.

But there was a connection there with pretty-boy Maddox, and Dan's order—his job—was to play on that connection. His mind raced. He could increase the number of their scenes together, look for opportunities in the editing. Let it evolve... naturally.

That way he would be keeping his word to Ava and keeping faith with the network. Simple.

Right.

'You sure you didn't miss any?' Dan smiled across the table.

Ava folded her serviette and placed it on her spotless plate

with no remorse. She'd soaked up the last traces of chilli sauce
with crusty bread. Frankly, she'd almost licked the bowl clean
while he watched, gobsmacked. Well, if he'd forgotten what a
woman eating looked like, that was on him.

'I grew up around a bunch of men. If you left it you lost it.'

Dan laughed. 'I know. I was there. I did warn you their
mussels were good.'

'You weren't kidding.' She patted a hand on her stomach.
'Fortunately I can work it off walking home. Which I should
do soon if I'm going to be on set on time tomorrow.'

Dan stood and moved around to slide her chair out. Thank
goodness his mood had lifted almost the minute they sat to eat
in the crowded café. She wasn't ready for another dose of surly
Arnot. Whatever had been bugging him when she left his office
seemed to have sorted itself.

'My shout,' Dan offered smoothly, sliding his gold credit
card across to the pretty cashier who'd been working hard all
night to get his attention. And failing.

'That's not necessary...' Ava reached out and stalled his
fingers with hers, embarrassed. This was hardly a date. Even
if her tingling fingers hadn't got that message. She curled them
safely into her fist.

'Corporate gold, Ava. It's on the network. It's the least
they can do.'

It sure was. Ava laughed and let AusOne buy her a meal.
Moments later they were walking away from the busy café
strip towards Dan's street. Hers now, too. She risked a glance
in his direction. He'd been nothing but charming throughout
dinner but was patently preoccupied. Several times she'd caught
him looking at her strangely, as though he were just about to
ask something. Then he'd drop those killer lashes and when he
looked up again the strangeness would be gone and they'd go
on talking—about the old days, Steve, her dad.

Even at one point her mum, whom Dan had mourned as if
she'd been his own. She practically had been. It was she who

had convinced Ava's father to let Dan stay as often as he needed to when he was a boy. So they knew he was at least sleeping in a safe place.

Dan took her elbow and steered her across the street between the cafés and the waterfront walk. A thousand lights sparkled across the harbour and cast a pretty glow.

'I lived for Friday nights back then,' he said, his eyes searching the water. 'Did you know that?'

Ava shook her head slightly. 'All I knew was you'd turn up on a Friday night like clockwork. There was a standing invitation.'

'Dinner at the Langes was the highlight of my week. So normal. I even got to play big brother for a night. I used to wish there were seven Fridays in a week.'

Ava flushed. There'd eventually come a point when she'd no longer been able to think of him platonically at all, and she'd barely been able to tolerate the meals which had grown increasingly frequent and increasingly awkward as her awareness of him had grown.

He kicked a stone to the side of the path. 'I missed those dinners after I left.'

Just the dinners, she told her racing heart. Not her. She mustn't read into it. 'Did you miss the surfing?'

She'd never forgiven herself for attacking his surfing that night on the beach. For sneering about his inability to make the pro circuit. He was still the best surfer she'd ever seen. Fearless. Inspirational.

Just part of the reason she'd been so crazy about him.

He studied her as they turned across a park towards the waterfront, his brows drawn together in a frown. 'No. If I hadn't given away surfing I never would have gone to uni. And if I hadn't studied business there's no way I'd have found my way here. We all grow up.' He sighed. 'But some days I'd just like to sit at that table again and flick peas at the kid across the table, you know?'

Ava smiled. 'You always missed.'

'You always ducked.' He stepped sideways suddenly and

nudged her with his hip, the way he'd used to when they were kids. She laughed to cover the zing that raced through her at the simple contact.

We all grow up.

And apart. The man he'd become was a hundred miles from the almost-man she remembered—the hotshot surfer whom everyone had expected to turn pro; the boy with a father but no family. She wondered whether she'd changed, too. The essential Ava.

'You've done well,' she said. 'Maybe it was all worth it?'

'I'd like to think so.'

'Word on the street is that you're the it-boy in television,' she said.

'"Word on the street"? What, you're hanging out with the boys in construction now?' His sideways glance was warm and close. Her heart kicked over.

Was he flirting with her?

'Okay, word in the catering van. I have ears. And Brant knows a lot about the business.'

He slowed as they approached Ava's little gate. She was happy to slow with him. She was enjoying this rare chance to connect with the *old* Daniel. No strings. No agendas.

'I don't want to talk about Maddox.' His brown eyes didn't quite meet hers.

'You don't like him?' she said.

'I didn't say that. He's very good at what he does, and he rates his socks off.'

'But?'

'But… I just don't want to talk about him. Not tonight.' He stopped under the stone arch which formed the gate to her little garden. His eyes were suddenly masked.

Tonight?

The word hung like a firework in the sky, all bright and hard to ignore. It made Ava suddenly aware of who and where they were: a man and a woman on a warm, moonlit night against the sparkling lights of Sydney. With a whole night ahead of them.

It almost made it possible to forget everything that stood between them.

He rested his forearm on the rammed-earth arch above her head, and it brought his body closer to hers. Her mouth dried as she looked up at him. He was still the best-looking man she knew. Brant might be beautiful, but it was a manufactured kind of beauty. The moonlight accentuated the line of Dan's jaw, his cheekbones and the ridge of his firm brow. The essential maleness of him stirred the same appreciation in her now as it always had.

Long before she should have been appreciating maleness. Her body quivered an alert. Time to change the subject.

'Did you ever sort things out with your father?' She winced as soon as the words were out of her mouth.

His whole body changed in an instant. His voice was curt in the quiet of the night. 'Next topic.'

Right.

'I guess some things don't change.' She didn't mean to say it aloud, and she barely did. Her body instinctively responded to the pain in his clipped words, wanting to heal him.

He looked at her steadily, his gaze softening and flitting over her face and shoulders before returning to her lips. Her heart fluttered helplessly. When they finally zeroed in on her eyes, his own had darkened two shades. Thick lashes swept down over them.

'While others change massively,' he murmured. 'How can I be standing here contemplating kissing the kid I flicked peas at?'

His hand dropped from the archway to rest gently on Ava's bare shoulder, his thumb toying with the thin straps of her summer dress where they crossed her suddenly scorching skin. Her heart pounded against her chest as though desperate for oxygen.

Her lungs certainly were.

This was a bad idea for so many reasons. But for the life of her she couldn't dredge up one.

This is Daniel. Beautiful, gorgeous, talented Daniel. And he was on the verge of kissing her. And she wanted that. Very badly.

How many kinds of masochist was she?

I will never be with you, Ava. His words echoed in her ears, forcing her body into action. She straightened against the little rendered archway and tried to think of something clever to say—something brilliant and witty and diverting—but she came up desperately short.

So she just stared at him, wary.

'God, Ava,' he breathed, dropping his hand. 'I'm sorry. I shouldn't have said that. You deserve more than your boss pawing you at your front door.'

Expensive aftershave mingled with the scent of raw man, seeping into her blood, racing narcotic-like through her veins. Waves lapped on the nearby waterfront. The aged archway pressed grittily into her shoulders. A phone rang somewhere nearby. She forgot to breathe.

I will never be with you, Ava. A voice screamed at her to remember, trying to make a dent in the bubble of awareness suddenly growing around them. She was supposed to move away. That would be the smart thing to do. But, God help her, only one part of her could move—and it wasn't her feet.

She straightened towards him, drawn like a magnet to his heat, and raised her eyes.

He bent cautiously towards her, his dark hair slipping down his forehead. A question burned bright in his gaze, but his lips separated just slightly as he zoomed in on hers. Such beautiful lips.

The phone pealed a second time. *Her* phone, inside the guesthouse. She ignored it. Dan's eyes held hers intently and his hands moved up to frame her face, strong fingers sliding behind her jaw and tipping her mouth towards him. The feel of his skin brushing against hers caused her legs to tremble and an impatient pulse kicked in deep inside her.

For the love of God, kiss me!

The phone shrilled a third time.

His mouth traced along her jaw just a millimetre above her flesh. He was scenting his way to his target, his breath hot against her skin. The excruciating trail robbed her of what precious little air remained in her lungs. Ava's fists clenched in his jacket to hold herself up.

And...finally...he touched his mouth to hers.

The charge that had built between them for over a decade was expelled the moment their mouths met. At the first caress of his soft, warm lips Ava jerked backwards into the rammed earth. With solid rock behind her there was nowhere else to go but ahead, into him. She closed the distance, sliding her mouth over his with a hungry moan.

Nine years of hunger. More.

'Ava...' he groaned against her lips. One large hand closed around her nape while the other slid to her waist, pulling her tight against him. Her own hands drifted deliriously against his broad chest as she tasted and tested and discovered his lips. Opening her mouth to him was as natural as the night going on around them.

Her face turned towards his like a moonflower straining towards its god. Dan splayed his legs slightly, to fit better against her small frame. Her head fell back as he stroked his tongue in and out of her mouth, tangling with hers, tracing the shape of her teeth on a long, pleasured growl. Every twist, every tangle was an erotic dance, increasing the voltage between them. The earth began to spin. Electricity buzzed, chemicals surged and Ava knew without a shadow of doubt that she would never experience a kiss quite like this again.

Ever.

It didn't matter that her legs gave way, because Dan held her so securely in his arms. Every part of him was rock-hard and, wrapped so close into him, she felt as though the two of them had simply melted into the stone archway.

In that moment she would have quite happily resided there with him for ever.

Dan's head lifted, his brown irises now liquid magma. Colour raced high in his jaw and his breathing was rough against her ear. 'Tell me to stop.'

Ava heaved in deep, ragged breaths, her thoughts jumbled. Why on earth would she stop something that felt this good?

I will never be with you...

Shut up, shut up! She trembled as endorphins surged through her system. She glanced at the door leading to the guestroom. The thought of Dan pressing down over her in the bedroom there, silhouetted against the giant moon was...*perfect*. But the chances of him sticking around afterwards? Of having anything more meaningful to offer her than one night?

Not high.

Still, she wasn't going to get another chance. She was lucky to be getting a second crack at her dream at all. And she was older now, and wise enough to know that there was no such thing as a happy ending. She glanced again at the door and verbalised her decision.

'Don't stop.'

Dan buried himself in her hair and pressed his lips behind her ear. Her legs sagged. He lifted her hard against him on a groan and turned towards the door.

Just then Ava's answering machine finally picked up the call in the guesthouse. Her father's voice carried out to where they stood. 'Hey, brat, it's me. Sorry, I've missed you...'

Dan froze, mid-step. Mid-kiss.

'Steve and I were cleaning the garage and we came across a pile of your old things. We were wondering if you wanted them? The only thing I recognise is your old blue bike, the one with the spokey-dokeys still on it.'

Dan's breath punched out of him. Ava looked into his pained face, his suddenly blank eyes where the fire had been.

No, no, no.... Her pathetic tugs towards the bedroom failed miserably. He tore his arm away from her and his head sagged towards his chest.

'Anyway, just give me a call and I'll talk you through it. Okay, talk soon. Love you.'

A beep, then silence. The only sound in the garden was them both heaving in a lungful of air. Ava took his hand in hers, her voice artificially, desperately light. She tugged...

But he resisted. Right up until that moment Ava had thought there might be something to salvage. That her chance might not have turned completely to ashes with one phone call.

He lifted tortured cold eyes and she knew.

Daniel Arnot was about to reject her...again.

CHAPTER SIX

EXCRUCIATING.

That was the only word for it. Ava wasn't sure what was worse—the moments where Daniel refused to meet her eyes, or those accidental moments where they did meet hers across the busy set, dark, shuttered, and glaring at her from under thick lashes.

Nice work, Lange. Sleeping with the man who broke your heart. Your boss. The fact she hadn't was only a matter of semantics and a few precious minutes. If not for her father's call…

It was all horribly out of character for her. She'd slept with an impressive total of two men in her whole life—hardly a football team. She'd not had the time or the interest for more. The first time had been all about getting it out of the way, shucking off the virgin label. And the second time… Well, he'd been nice, funny and interested, and she'd thought that might be enough. It had been affection more than attraction on her part.

But she'd sure been attracted two nights ago. She'd never felt such a yearning. Stupid word, but it fitted perfectly.

She could only wonder what she'd be feeling today if the phone had been set to silent.

'Ava?' Brant appeared beside her, and she welcomed the distraction. 'Care to run some lines while they change the set-up?'

Brant knew next to nothing about plants—although he was a quick study—so he rarely deviated from the text provided by the show's writers. The cues were his anchors, and so, for his sake, Ava tried to memorise them. If she was going to go roaming freely off-script to talk about her passion, the least she could do was give Brant his in and out points.

He thrust some crisp, clean pages at her. She took them cautiously. 'What are these?'

'Rewrites.'

'They've rewritten the segments?' She had one to-camera segment today, and Brant had one. Both complicated set-ups. Between that was some serious design time. Now she had to run new lines.

'Nope, merged segments. We're doubling up in each one.'

Both of us? She glanced at the pages and saw the writers had added a line or two for each of them in the other's segment. At least she wouldn't be standing there like a dunce while Brant presented. 'Why?'

'Orders from our friendly neighbourhood producer. Shall we?' He popped her on the shoulder with his rolled-up pages and smiled.

She sighed. 'Sure. Let's use the stairwell, where it's quiet.'

They were eight storeys high on the roof of a small business block on the edge of the Sydney CBD. A rooftop seething with tradesmen, television crew and assorted *Urban Nature* work crew. She'd designed this rooftop habitat months ago, such was the preparation which went into some of these rehab jobs. To Ava it *was* rehabilitation: turning grey concrete messes into natural spaces with soul. She'd relished the challenge of taking this barren man-made rooftop and softening it with native grasses and succulents, running it through with timber boardwalks.

All day long they'd drawn curious looks from the windows of the factories that overlooked their worksite. Ava wasn't sure what interested them more, the transformation of the roof space into a lush garden, or the cameras and obvious television activity. Or possibly the presence of pin-up boy Brant. She'd like to think the former.

'You sure you don't want to use your trailer?' Brant gave her one of his winning smiles as she hauled open the door to the infrequently used stairs leading from the rooftop. 'It'll only take a second to get there.'

Ava frowned. Was he trying to get her alone in her trailer? The way he was leaning on the doorframe oh-so-casually, smiling down on her, cajoling… But there was something not quite authentic about it. She looked around them. And smiled.

'You don't want to get your trousers dirty.' She knew she was right. The stairs were caked in years of commercial grime.

Brant glanced over his shoulder and then pursued her into the stairwell, pulling the door closed behind them. 'It's filthy in here,' he whispered urgently. 'And Carrie will have my ass if I trash another set of trousers.'

Ava laughed. 'You are such a princess, Maddox.'

He whacked her harder with his script pages. Ava laughed more. It was getting tougher not to like him. 'Fine, we'll adjourn to my office—where we can rehearse in the splendour to which you've obviously become accustomed.'

Brant smiled as they turned to the stairs and slung one arm around her shoulder. 'You're a good sort, Lange. I owe you one.'

'Going somewhere?'

Cool air was sucked in as the rooftop door suddenly opened behind them. Ava twisted to follow the sound.

'Dan.' She cringed at the breathiness of her own voice, and the subtle lift of Brant's eyebrow told her he hadn't missed it. Defensiveness surged through her. 'We're off to rehearse our surprise new lines. Your doing, I understand?'

His chocolate gaze was steady. 'I wanted to try working you two together more this episode. Give you a chance to get to know each other.' He looked pointedly at Brant's arm around her shoulder then looked at Ava. 'Perhaps it was unnecessary?'

Brant dropped his arm, but not in much of a hurry. 'I'm not complaining. I think we make a good pair, don't you, Ava?'

She struggled to muster a smile. The Dan she remembered

had never switched it on and off quite so effectively, but he was standing scowling darkly at her now. Two nights ago he'd had his tongue in her mouth.

For the first time since moving to Sydney she felt out of her depth. Was this how things were done in Dan's high-rise world? Treating people this way? She wasn't cut out for it if it was. But she'd be damned before she'd let him see that. She took her cue from Brant, adopted an unconcerned veneer and smiled. Her best TV-host sparkler.

'Absolutely.'

Without a backward glance, she continued down the stairs to the top-floor elevators, below which was the safety of her mobile office. The one place she knew Dan would not enter un-invited. Since gifting it to her it in the first place he hadn't set so much as a foot across its threshold. It was her sanctuary.

She felt his eyes on her until she pushed through the heavy door onto the top-floor landing. She glanced up at him just before she passed through. He stared down the stairwell as dark and gloomy as a storm cloud.

One that was threatening to break.

Yesterday's work had been brutal, but productive. They'd shot all the 'before' segments, showing the scope of the barren rooftop canvas they would be working with, and overnight construction fairies had come in and laid the entire space with a chequerboard of timbers and subterranean drainage to help keep the tonne of introduced soil on the rooftop from becoming waterlogged.

They'd captured that work in time-lapse, so that there'd be no illusions that it was an easy job, but for the production crew the hard work started now.

Dan roamed the set, thinking about how long it had been since he'd been hands-on in production. Or since he'd worked outdoors. It felt good.

Really good.

The stairwell door opened and Ava and Brant emerged from

below, kidding around with a sound technician and entirely relaxed at the start of the day. But the moment her eyes found his they dulled and the gorgeous smile faltered.

Damn. He'd done that. He'd done exactly what he'd promised James Lange he'd never do.

Hurt Ava.

Twice. And now he'd been complicit in setting her up with a lech. The worst possible type of man for her. Okay, the *second* worst possible type of man. Maddox had yet to paw her in her own front garden. Dan glared at the blond pretty-boy and the way he smiled at Ava.

Give him time…

On a curse, he marched over to where Ava poured coffee from the makeshift servery. 'Ava. Can I have a minute?' he barked at her.

She fumbled the coffee she was pouring, and then placed it down carefully before turning to him. Silent. Not giving an inch. He probably deserved at least that. The caterer raised his eyebrows and turned politely away, but Dan knew he wouldn't miss a thing. He drew her away from prying ears.

'About Maddox and you…' The rest hung awkwardly.

Ava raised her eyebrows, clearly impatient. He instantly felt about eight years old, facing his father. The man with a special talent for making a boy feel stupid. But on this occasion he was doing just fine on his own.

'The two of you are…getting on well.' He struggled to pull the frost from his voice

Ava shook her head and took a deep breath. 'Yes, we are. Isn't that what all the rewrites have been about? Building rapport?'

'On screen, Ava. Not off.'

Her sharp mind raced. 'There is no "off screen" with Brant and I. What are you accusing me of?'

'I'm not accusing you. I'm just reminding you. I don't want any interpersonal issues affecting production.' *You stinking hypocrite, Arnot.*

Ava glared at him. 'Brant's not the man you seem to think—'

'I know exactly what kind of man he is. He's not the right sort for you.'

'Oh, really?' Sparks practically shot from her eyes. 'And what kind of man *is* right for me?'

'Someone who challenges you. Someone with half a brain.'

'Only half? You flatter me.' She shot him a contemptuous look and turned to walk away.

'Don't.' He reached out and spun her towards him. The caterer abandoned all pretence of not listening in. Dan pulled her entirely out of earshot. 'Don't look at me like that.'

She blazed at him. 'Like what?'

'Like I've done something to you that you weren't a willing party to. You kissed me back.'

'I thought your plan was just to pretend that never happened?'

'It happened, and my bet is we've both been thinking about it,' he said.

'But not talking about it, apparently.'

'What's to talk about? It was a mistake.'

Doe eyes rounded in her pale face. 'Is that a fact?'

'You're Steve's little sister—not to mention you're the talent on my show. And we have history.' He stacked the excuses so high he could hardly see over them. 'You and I hooking up was never going to be anything but inappropriate.'

'*Inappropriate?* That's a very politically correct way of putting it.'

'You want me to say *mistake* again?'

Colour roared into her face. 'The kind of man that suits me or doesn't is none of your business, Daniel Arnot,' she raged. 'My relationship with Brant is also none of your business. AusOne's bought my face and my expertise. Nothing more. Now, if you don't mind, I have work to do.' She twisted free and marched off towards the rest of the crew.

A choice curse crossed his lips.

He'd stuffed that up royally. All he'd wanted to do was warn her, take some of the wind out of Maddox's sails. His gut was festering like an ulcer watching them together. Smiling at each other, sharing private jokes. Sharing private anything.

It galled him almost as much to watch it as it did to know that she was playing right into the network's hands. What had happened to the professional self-respect she had gone on about? He'd barely had to give her a nudge and she was falling right in with a sleaze like Maddox. So easy.

Dan frowned. Ava wasn't easy. The woman was pure hard work.

Despite what they'd shared three nights ago, Dan knew in his heart that it wasn't her style to sleep with someone on the first date—it hadn't even been a date, he had to remind himself—so she wasn't about to go tumbling into bed with Maddox.

Not straight away, anyway.

But later? When she'd got to know him a little? Would she remain blind to the real man beneath the glamour? The man who liked his women fast and free? Who left them even faster? Just the thought of Maddox's hands on Ava's body made his skin burn. He unclenched his balled fists and glanced at the red welts across his palm where his nails had cut in.

Not Ava.

He felt like a fraud. Pushing Ava towards Maddox with one hand and pulling her away with the other. He'd jeopardised his job, just now, trying to warn her off. But he'd underestimated her tenacity and her loyalty. Or maybe he'd underestimated Maddox and his skill. Either way, the result was the same.

Maddox one, Arnot nil.

Damn.

CHAPTER SEVEN

THERE were less than ten minutes to crunch time. The first show of the new season was airing across Australia at seven-thirty p.m. Ava kept telling herself it didn't matter if she did well—that it wasn't important to excel, she only had to be reasonable. Maintaining her professional credibility was what was important, and the designs. Not being the world's best television presenter.

But another part of her wanted to do well. For herself and for Dan, if she was being honest, to help make the show the success he so desperately wanted it to be. She was still mad with him, furious that he'd brought Brant into the stupid mixed-up mess that was their friendship, but despite all that her lingering feelings for him still drove her to do well for his sake.

Lingering, Ava? Or returning?

Dan entered the crowded bar on the ground floor of AusOne and, judging by his suit, he'd come straight down from his office. He scanned the room immediately, until his eyes met hers for less than a heartbeat before he looked away. But his room-scanning ceased. He immediately became engaged in conversation with a few of the mid-level executive types from the network.

She fought her natural inclination to think he might have been looking for her. Probably gearing up for battle. The past few days had been uncomfortable enough—avoiding each other's eyes, the stony silences.

'Nervous?' Carrie, resplendent in a peacock-blue skirt and with the sensational make-up you would expect of a professional, shoved a glass of juice into Ava's hand as she slid into the booth next to her. Ava regretted her choice of a simple summer dress and not even eye make-up.

'It feels weird to be worrying about anything more than how the design comes across on television.'

'The design and you will both be fabulous.' Carrie squeezed her arm.

'I hate this part.' A bright-eyed Brant slid into the booth beside Ava, then waved Carrie around to his other side. 'If we go down in flames then I'd like to do it sandwiched between two beautiful women.'

Carrie laughed and obliged, shuffling over to Brant's left. 'Nice suit,' she said to him, sipping her drink innocently.

'Spotless, you'll notice.'

Their typical banter helped take her mind off the moment to come. She looked at her watch and swallowed. Two minutes to launch. Dan moved to stand under the widescreen television and called for hush.

'In just over sixty seconds the second season of *Urban Nature* will hit living rooms all over the country,' he announced. 'Advance audiences have liked it, some have loved it, but we've all seen shows rate well on test and then sink on air.'

Ava swallowed. He looked so calm, utterly confident. She knew he had to be anything but, and her heart went out to him. She reined it in.

'This won't be one of them. We've pulled a good show together, folks.' He raised his beer in salute. 'To all of you who've worked so hard, and to what we hope will be AusOne's biggest new hit…to *Urban Nature*.'

The crowd echoed his toast, and the sound of clinking glasses resounded through the stylish bar. Carrie and Brant touched glasses to her left. Ava looked up and met Dan's eyes, and he raised his bottle of designer beer in silent acknowledgement and then brought it to his lips as the lights started to dim. She couldn't get her eyes off those lips. She knew, firsthand, how that bottle was feeling. Only when the room got dark and the titles for *Urban Nature* began to air was she able to drag her focus off his mouth.

She let her breath out slowly in the darkness of the now quiet room. The opening titles finished and the show began. Brant's handsome face, even better-looking on television, beamed out at them. His voice was warm and rich as he introduced the audience to the *Urban Nature* concept and his new co-host and designer, Ava Lange.

Ava saw her own face fill the screen. She looked far more together than she remembered feeling; the editing team had done a fantastic job of placing overlay footage at those places where her composure had faltered. She and Brant worked well together, and it was clear immediately that there was a whole team working on the install.

A load lifted from her as she realised the network hadn't pulled any swifties regarding the true number of people working on the installs. No one would be in any doubt about how many people it really took to create the finished garden. She'd heard on the grapevine that Dan had negotiated ruthlessly to affect those changes with the network this season. *Her* season. Would he have made the same call had she not put such a priority on maintaining integrity?

Her credibility was thus far intact. She settled in to watch, her drink untouched.

Six minutes later the show broke for the first of many commercials. Ava glanced nervously around the room as the lights rose and saw nothing but smiles. Gradually the silence morphed into a murmur of excitement. Then a throng.

'I'd say we're onto a winner, hon,' Brant said, beside her. 'You're quite amazing up there. Completely...' He struggled for the right word.

'Vibrant.' Dan spoke from immediately behind their booth, and Ava leapt at his unexpected closeness. 'You've both come up trumps. Congratulations.'

'We should say the same to you.' Brant tipped his head in courteous acknowledgement.

Dan slid onto the seat by Ava's side, leaned over and clacked his beer against the one offered by Brant. The move pressed his body against hers.

Her blood thrummed. The booth was small, and the addition of Dan only made it smaller. His heat soaked into her and she struggled not to think about the many places where he was touching her. His thigh, his hip, his long muscled arm. Fire rose in her cheeks and she squirmed. *Not* thinking about touching only made her flash back to the other night. Something she was trying hard not to do. How those powerful arms had felt crushing her to him. How his hands had dwarfed her face as he cupped it. How he'd spread his thighs to bring his mouth closer to hers. Oh, that mouth....

'How are you feeling?' Dan's breath tickled her ear as he leaned in close to speak.

She nearly yelped. The question encompassed more than just the show; she could see it in the smoky depths of his eyes. Was this an olive branch? Lord, she wanted it to be. She missed him, pure and simple. The kisses had been to die for, but she wasn't sure they were worth the arguments or the days of frosty silent treatment afterwards. The hurtful, lingering silences.

For the first time she began to understand why he had left back when she was sixteen. The cleanest cut.

'Pleased so far. It's good, Dan.'

Warmth flashed across his expression and she struggled to read it. Was it pleasure at her compliment or that she'd accepted his peace offering? Whatever, she found it hard not to bask in the hint of warmth in eyes that had been arctic for days.

'I haven't seen you around at the house.' She leaned in close, keeping her voice low in the hubbub. Only a trusted few knew she and Dan were sharing a roof. The move only increased the number of places their bodies touched. Her nerve-endings sang. 'Where've you been?'

'I've worked late quite a bit this week. End of financial year reports, market analyses.'

Avoiding you, he might as well have said.

But she was no different. How had she known Dan wasn't home? Because she'd worked late every night, tucked up in her Winnebago in the car bay next to his empty one. There was something sad and lonely about that—the two of them burning the midnight oil, working towards the same goal, yet in complete isolation from each other.

'Dan, I—'

The lights dimmed again and a hush fell in the room. He threw her a long look as he slid out of the booth. In the sinking darkness his fingers brushed against hers and then he was gone. She stared at the giant monitor but saw nothing. The tingle in her fingers from where he'd accidentally touched her spread like spilled champagne.

If it had been accidental?

They'd done it. Everyone in the room held their breath until the final name rolled on the credits, and then a rousing cheer went through the bar. The show was good—better than good—and everyone knew it.

Drinks flowed and the conversation grew deafening as excited people tried to talk over other excited people. The energy in the room quadrupled, and Ava got caught up in the maelstrom of sheer goodwill. After the first couple of shouted compliments—which she struggled to accept without flushing—it became easier to smile, to receive the good wishes with grace.

The editing team were the heroes of the night, their work being the major contributor to the pace and atmosphere of the programme. They'd lifted it from the realm of commercial lifestyle television to somewhere higher, and they'd taken everyone involved in its creation right along with them. It was nothing like their competition.

Ava didn't realise she was searching the room until her eyes found their target. Across the bar, Dan flipped his cell open and answered. He turned half away and plugged his other ear with a finger, as if that would lessen the cacophony. Ava watched him closely, trying to guess what he was saying. His eyes widened, and then closed briefly before he lowered the phone. But he didn't snap it shut.

He called again for quiet, and had to employ the help of several others when he was roundly ignored by the masses. Eventually the noise level reluctantly dropped. He spoke quickly to his assistant producer and turned away.

'Preliminary figures have us at eight!' the assistant whooped.

Another cheer, more whistling and clinking of glasses, a second round of backslapping. Brant had warned her anything above six on the rating scale was good news. An eight was fantastic news. She looked around to congratulate Dan, just in time to see him slipping out of the bar, the phone still glued to his ear. She pushed towards him, but not fast enough.

In the end her whispered congratulations smacked against the door he disappeared through.

'Say that again, Bill?'

Dan slumped against the wall of the lift, his pleasure at rating an eight short-lived.

'They were every bit as popular with the real audience as they were with the test one. We want you to ramp up the Ava/Brant thing. Put some spin on it.'

'Spin.' The word was like a curse.

'Maddox has made some bad choices in his career. Not in terms of his work, God knows, but his personal life. The number of times the network has had to bail him out of one seedy bar or another, or pay off some skank who's trying to make the headlines… Someone like Ava could be the best thing for his reputation. Put a bit of distance on those bad choices.'

Who cares about Maddox? Dan closed his eyes. 'She won't do it.'

'Persuade her. Convince her. Lie to her for all I care. Just make it happen. I want apple-pie Ava Lange and bad-boy Brant Maddox firmly connected in people's minds this time next week. I don't care if they're out buying milk—you make it look like they're scouting for a home.'

'And if I say no?'

The silence was ugly. But Dan could play that game; he'd been raised on it. He waited Kurtz out.

'I'm giving you first refusal here, Dan. Out of respect. But if you won't do it I'll task it to the spin department. I don't care who gives it to me just as long as I get it. Lange and Maddox are the next it-couple on the East Coast.'

Dan thought furiously. He'd seen what the sharks from PR had done before. No way was he throwing them Ava. But that meant he had to work her over himself. Kurtz was counting on that. This stank of a set-up.

Kurtz had just declared war.

Was this how evil did its thing? No shadowy horned creature standing at a crossroads at midnight. Just a whole series of moments like this one, with choices that could be justified if you talked long enough. When someone asked him to compromise just a little piece more of his soul.

On those occasions, Dan just looked to the thing inside him that surged in his gut and drove him like a wild-eyed racehorse. A vivid memory of a sneering voice and a brutal hand and the damage that both could inflict to a young boy.

But under no circumstances was he throwing Ava to the PR sharks. He took a breath and ripped off another chunk of his soul. 'I'll take care of it.'

'Excellent.' Kurtz didn't even bother to disguise the gloat. 'Let me know if there's anything I can do.'

Dan slammed his phone shut on the mirrored wall of the lift, his mind racing. Publicity was essential to a programme's success, and it would naturally focus on the two hosts to some degree. His job now was to make sure that he could spin the spin.

Control the beast.

But that meant controlling Ava. Good luck with that! If she found out about this, there was every chance she'd end up hating him. If she didn't already hate him for running out on her the other night.

She'd never believe for a second that both were for her protection.

He shook his head. Was there really that much difference between him and Maddox? His father had always said he was as faithless as his cheating mother, and in this at least good ol' Pop might have been on the money. He visualised Ava's beautiful face in the bar downstairs, the trust that had flowered so easily after a few days of hostilities between them. Then he imagined betraying that trust.

If this was going to work he'd have to depersonalise things. Sever those golden rare threads of attraction that had started to string between him and Ava. It was an all too seductive luxury that he just couldn't afford.

He swore under his breath and sent the lift to the foyer.

'Want to share a ride home?'

Home. The word sounded so comfortable coming out of Dan's mouth. Almost possible. Ava let herself be guided out of the bar by the hand at her back, squeezing past the still celebrating crew and network personnel. The warm night air kissed her skin as they emerged onto the street. Dan glanced around for a taxi.

'How do you feel about the ferry?' Ava asked, waving onwards the taxi that had spotted them. 'I could use the walk.' *And some uninterrupted time with you.* Ten minutes to Circular Quay, fifteen crossing the harbour, and another ten strolling home from the Neutral Bay pier. Plenty of time for what she was hoping to say.

It was time she laid a few demons to rest. And established a few boundaries.

Dan set off on an incomprehensible route towards the quay, through bustling night streets lit mostly by the fluorescent shop-fronts and fast-food signs which lined them. It wasn't yet ten o'clock, and the city still bustled with diners, shoppers, sight-seers and late workers heading home. He cut confidently through all the passers-by just a step ahead of her, making her path effortless. He was so comfortable in this city, such a natural part of it.

'Okay, Ava?'

The man could sure read her. 'I was just thinking that I could drive a tank through the main street in Flynn's Beach this time of night and not see a soul.'

His lips quirked at the memory. 'Different world. Each has its merits.'

They emerged onto George Street and turned towards the Sydney Harbour Bridge in all its glory against the night sky. They moved with the crowd surging towards Circular Quay, where a fleet of large green ferries came and went like a rapidly changing tide, taking people across the harbour and up-river.

Dan slowed and stepped in beside her. 'It took me a while to get used to Sydney time. It works differently to the rest of the country.'

Ava looked at the throng of people around her and shook her head. 'I'm struggling with the idea of six months, and you've been here six years.'

'You get used to it. It gets in your blood.'

'I thought you'd have picked a beach property? To be close to the surf?'

His glance flicked to the bridge. 'I needed a clean break from surfing. It wasn't something I could just do casually. But I couldn't face the idea of watching other people do it out of my window.'

A clean break. He seemed to have so little difficulty making that kind of cut. She visualised his favourite surfboard and wondered if Old Faithful felt as strongly about his amputate-the-limb approach.

Surfing. His father. *Her.*

The throng paused momentarily at an intersection, and then surged ahead as the crossing lights changed. Dan directed her carefully, with a hand at her lower back. As warm as she already was on the typical Australian summer evening, his palm seared its print on her skin through her light dress.

At the quay, ferries came and went, servicing the many luxury properties along Sydney's extensive waterfront. Dan and Ava broke away from the general crowd and crossed to where the Neutral Bay ferry sat waiting for passengers travelling across-harbour to the ritzy suburb. The lights of the Opera House cast an eerie glow.

Dan led the way to the enclosed upper deck, close to an open window. Fresh salty air streamed in as the massive engines roared to life and they rumbled out into the harbour.

Ava settled in for the fifteen-minute trip and did her best to ignore the heat surging from the man next to her. It wasn't easy. He'd shrugged off his jacket so only the thin cotton of a designer shirt stood between her and the hard expanse of his chest.

That chest. Two deep breaths were barely enough to get her composure on an even keel.

'Feeling okay?' he asked.

'I'm just…puffed out from the walk.'

'Yep. No one strolls in Sydney.'

She shifted uncomfortably on the green plastic seating. 'Why did you come here?' she asked.

'This was where the work was.'

'There was work at home.'

His eyes darted to the lights of the city, receding behind them. 'I couldn't be who I needed to be in Flynn's Beach.'

'Who was that?'

Waves crashed relentlessly on the ferry's bow. 'Someone new. I needed to reinvent myself.'

'What was wrong with your old self?'

'Nothing. He's still in here somewhere. But to do what I wanted—want—to do, I needed a blank canvas. I needed to be anonymous.'

She looked at the city where he must have known practically no one six years ago. 'You certainly got that. Did you not feel that old Dan could make it here?'

His fists clenched and unclenched on his lap. 'I was barely more than a kid, Ava. Dan-the-Man—king of the small town waves. How seriously was that guy going to be taken in Sydney?'

'So you just killed him off? Cut him off, just like surfing?'

Just like me?

His jaw clenched. 'Having nothing, knowing no one, helped me focus only on my goal. My career.' His eyes found the blinking lights of the far shore and home. 'I wouldn't have any of this if I hadn't taken the risk.'

'It doesn't mean you'd have nothing. You'd just have had different things. Why do you want this particularly?'

He spun round to pin her with his eyes. 'Same reason you do. To be the best. To be the first. You create gardens; I create television shows.'

'I design landscapes because I want to help change people's attitudes to nature. Why do you want to create television shows, specifically?'

She couldn't fault his drive or question his success. Even if some of his methods didn't seem ideal, if the gossips were to be believed, Daniel Arnot was on the fast track to running his own network one day in the not too distant future. That sort of success didn't come without a cost.

But did that have to include his soul?

'Because I want to be...' He dropped his eyes and his voice. 'Because it's important to me to succeed.'

'I get that. But why the mammoth drive? Why do you burn with it?'

He nailed her with his gaze. 'Because I want to be better than *him*.'

A tiny light came on in her mind. His father. Mitchell Arnot owned a small chain of garages along the southern coast. He was one of Flynn's Beach's leading businessmen.

She frowned. 'I think it's safe to say you've eclipsed his success ten times over, Dan.'

'Eclipsing is not enough. I'm aiming for total annihilation.'

Well! That was a conversation-stopper. If not for the agony in his eyes she'd almost be afraid of the hate also burning there. Ava had wondered what had driven Dan away from his father, but her parents had never shared. She'd gleaned a few things from the town gossips—a hippy mother who left him when he was barely walking, and a difficult relationship with his father ever since—but nothing that warranted that level of response.

Lord, a public ferry was so *not* the place for this discussion. She leaned forward and lowered her voice. 'What did he do to you?' she whispered.

'That's none of your business.'

He might as well have slapped her in the face.

He swore and barely met her eyes, speaking softly. Pained. 'I can't talk about this with you, Ava.'

She willed herself to be patient. Not to react to the hurt. 'Have you talked about this with anyone?'

The silence stretched. The ferry chugged. 'Your father. He helped me to…moderate…my feelings.'

This bruised, vicious drive was *moderated*? What on earth had Mitchell Arnot done to his son? Ava covered her shock. 'That explains a lot. You two were always so close.'

Dan just nodded.

'Do you miss my dad?' she asked.

'Yeah. I do. I tried to stay in touch for a while, but it got…hard.'

She remembered how worried her father had been when

Dan had moved to Sydney. When he'd dropped out of all contact. How hurt. Trying to disguise it from a still-grieving Ava. 'Too hard to pick up the phone?'

Dan glared at her. 'You were just a kid, Ava. You don't understand.'

'What?' Her eyes burned into his. 'What don't I understand?'

He seemed to pick his words carefully. 'Not everyone got to have a fairytale childhood.'

'Fairytale? I watched my mother die of cancer when I was eight years old.'

Dan swore. 'I know. But you had your father and Steve. I had no one.'

I *have* no one. Was that what he meant? 'You chose to go. Nobody forced you,' she pointed out.

He burned to say something more; it was in the tightness of his lips, the intensity of his eyes. But he turned away and stared down at the watery depths passing by. They ploughed onwards in silence, and Ava grew hypnotised by the wash of the waves against the bow, the smell of the salt water on the warm night air. The rush of her thoughts.

She'd never got anywhere with her questions about Dan's family, so eventually she'd just stopped asking. Stopped thinking about it. She'd accepted Dan as part of the furniture—part of the family. Even now. No matter how much time had passed. No matter how he'd hurt her.

Or that they'd kissed.

But he still wouldn't share himself with her. Not as he'd shared himself with her father. She'd wanted to talk about the kiss tonight, to boldly go... But he suddenly seemed further away than ever, though he was only inches from her.

And so she sat, listening to the whoosh of the waves as it melded with the steady thrum of blood past her ears.

She'd waited nine years. She could wait a little longer.

* * *

As they swung against the pier at Neutral Bay, Dan stood and offered Ava his hand. She placed hers tentatively in it. As he pulled her up, the ferry lurched against the row of tyres mounted to the jetty and he caught her as she stumbled, wrapping one arm across her protectively.

Immediately her senses thrilled. Images, memories and feelings from the other night rushed in, exalting at being released. His lips. His warmth. The hungry press of his body. She slid one hand between them and braced against his chest to steady herself, hungry to feel again the particular hard softness that was Dan. She suddenly realised the whole night had been leading to this moment in her mind. She peered up at him through a veil of lashes.

Holding her breath.

He watched the boat's docking with interest, and his arms dropped from around her as soon as the ferry's turbulence eased. She straightened, frowning and not a little disappointed, and followed him to the exit.

He was entirely unaffected. More fascinated by the boat landing, apparently, than by the woman in his arms.

Ava trailed desolately down the stairs to the gangway. They crossed the pier and walked out into the quiet, late-night streets of Neutral Bay. Three or four others disembarked behind them and then dissolved into the darkness of the night, heading for their own homes.

Dan hooked his jacket over one shoulder and buried the other hand in his trouser pocket. *No chance of further accidental contact there.* Or intentional. Ava's lips tightened. She wondered if her carefully rehearsed speech would be wasted. He hardly seemed eager for a repeat performance of the other night—perhaps her boundary-setting would be unnecessary. But home, their separate dwellings, was only a few more minutes away.

It was now or never.

'Dan,' she began, risking a glance at him, 'about the other night…'

He slowed fractionally—all the evidence Ava got that he'd heard her. His eyes remained silently fixed on the luxury street they walked along.

Frustration leaked out between her words. 'Are we never going to discuss it?'

Silent seconds ticked by before he sighed and pulled his fingers from his pocket to drag them through his thick hair. 'It shouldn't have happened. It was inappropriate in so many ways.'

Ava's lips tightened. *There was that word again.* 'Because you're my boss?'

'And a friend of your brother's. Your father's. I'm practically a brother to you.'

Her head snapped up at that. How long was he going to hide behind that one? She scoffed. 'You don't think they'd approve?'

'*I* don't approve, Ava. You and I getting hot and heavy is a bad idea all round.'

Ava nursed the tiny hurt his words caused and forced herself not to dwell on just how hot and how heavy he might be, towering over her. Her blood rushed.

'Then why did we?' His shrug was no answer. It irritated Ava enough to make her careless. 'You started it, Dan.'

He hissed at her choice of phrase. 'Can you hear yourself? You might as well be wearing plaits and braces. Not exactly an image I find attractive at my age.'

At any age. She'd been there the first time. 'You're hardly an old man, Dan. And I'm twenty-five. All grown up.' She clamped her jaw hard.

'Physically, maybe—'

'Emotionally as well. I'm a different person to the girl I was then.' Belatedly, Ava remembered she was supposed to be arguing him *out* of any further physical interaction between them. But the sheer injustice of what he was saying stuck in her gut. 'If I'm able to separate boy-Dan from man-Dan, then why can't you separate the girl I was from the woman I am now?'

He stopped hard and blazed dark eyes at her. 'You had a head start, Ava. I was already a man and you were always just a kid.'

The old hurt surged to the fore. 'You're overlooking one important point, Dan. *You* came on to *me*. You kissed me. No one held a gun to your head.'

His lips tightened, then parted in an almost-snarl. 'You want me to say it, Ava? Fine. You *have* grown up. You have a fantastic body and you know how to use it. You were using it on me that night, in all that moonlight, and just for a second I thought why the hell not?'

Ava sucked in an outraged breath to protest but he bullied onwards.

'Hey, I never pretended to be a saint. I got carried away in the moment, just like you did. Thank God your father called when he did, or we might be having a very different conversation right now.'

Outrage shook her hands, and she tucked them behind her. Unfulfilled tears ached in her throat. 'I did not get carried away—'

Sharp eyes challenged her. 'You meant for it to happen, then?'

'No!'

'So you got carried away.' He loomed over her. 'Put away the righteous indignation, Ava. We were both curious and we tested the waters. End of story.'

Suddenly what they'd shared sounded so...*filthy*. She blazed silently at him, determined not to let one angry tear spill over. She wouldn't give him the satisfaction. She turned and stalked off along the leafy street.

His quiet challenge followed. 'Or were you hoping for a second go-around?'

She spun around to face him. 'You must be joking!'

'Wasn't that where this was going? *Can we talk about it, Dan?*' His impersonation of her was insulting.

'No!' She moved off again, furious.

'Then where's the problem? You were going to tell me it won't happen again. I certainly don't want it to happen again. I think we're actually on the same page here.'

She turned with dangerous deliberation and marched straight towards him, fast enough that he actually faltered back a step when she poked him in the chest.

'What happened to you, Dan? What happened to the clever, troubled young man who used to patch me up when I fell off my surfboard? The boy my mother opened her home to?'

The boy I gave my heart to. He didn't answer, staring at her with intense heat. Well, if he had nothing to say, then, by God, she was going to have her turn.

'I thought I'd lost him that day on the beach, when you ripped my heart out without a second thought, and then in your office, when you brought in your legal muscle to force me into accepting your stinking deal. But then the other night I got a glimpse of the young man I remembered, and I wondered whether he wasn't just buried, deep in there—' she poked his chest hard '—under six years of loneliness.'

He stepped back again.

'But that Daniel—my Daniel—would never speak to someone the way you just did. Not someone they once called a friend.' Impotent rage shook her voice and she swiped at a single tear that had leaked out, furious with herself for allowing it to escape.

'That's the problem, Ava. I was never *yours*. And you always did have me on too high a pedestal.' He flung his arms out wide. 'Welcome to reality, honey.'

'Your reality, maybe. Not mine.' She heaved in an angry breath. 'I'll stick out my six months because I said I would, and because, unlike you—' she poked him again '—I still value the integrity my father raised me to have.'

'Leave your father out of this.'

She started retreating from him, eager that he wouldn't miss her parting words. 'I hope it's worth it, Dan—your success, your high and mighty career. Because I know Dad would be ashamed to see the man you've become. *I'm* ashamed of you.'

With that, she spun around and sprinted off into the night rather than shed one more tear in front of him.

Coward, coward, *coward*.

Dan cursed himself all the way into his immaculate home. Spotless, expensive and empty.

I was never yours. Such lies. He'd been hers the moment she stood up to him and his lawyers in his office. But he'd said the one thing he knew would force some space between them. And it had worked. For a few minutes there, on the ferry, he'd felt her drawing closer, felt the threads of attraction strengthening and tangling. He'd been crazy to think the two of them could have any kind of normal relationship.

She was too much a part of his history. She knew all his buttons. And he wore down too quickly with the distraction of her closeness, her smell. Relating to her more like lovers than friends.

Almost-lovers.

For a few tantalising minutes on the ferry he'd let his guard relax, cracked the radiator cap and let some of the incredible pressure he'd been holding onto out into the atmosphere. But Ava was the one person in the world he couldn't afford to get close to.

What the hell kind of choice was that? Between the girl he'd promised to protect and the career that was his whole reason for being.

But then the ferry had sent Ava crashing into his arms, and one glance at her flushed face and parted lips and he'd *known* he was in trouble. It had taken all his will-power to keep his own face impassive, to give nothing away.

To take his hands off her.

She'd been braver than he was, broaching the subject of the kiss directly, and with such an accent of hope in her voice. One gutsy woman—but still entirely transparent. He'd had no choice but to come out swinging.

Dan reached into his stainless steel fridge and snatched out a frosty beer, twisting the cap off and hurling it across the room into the gleaming sink. He downed one-third of the bottle in one miserable swallow and then slammed it onto the bench, his eyes watering.

He hadn't worked himself halfway into the grave for six years to throw it all away now. He would not rest until his father knew exactly how successful his son had grown up to be.

Without him.

Mitchell Arnot was a big fish in a small pond. A pompous, ignorant fish, with all the parenting skills of a sea-jelly. Being able to get a transient hippy pregnant did not a good parent make. And Dan had paid his whole childhood for the sins of his free-spirit mother, who had skipped out when he was barely out of nappies.

He might have been beloved by the folk of Flynn's Beach, but Mitchell Arnot was loathed by his son and the feeling was entirely mutual. He'd got more love and understanding from the Langes than he'd ever got from either of his real parents.

The only useful thing his father had done was taunt him about being a beach bum. That had sparked a passionate desire to succeed that had quickly flared into an all-consuming bushfire. And he was going to ride this train to the end of the line if it killed him. To show Mitchell Arnot the true definition of success.

He had a job to do. And today's compromise, as much as it clawed in his gut, was that he needed to throw some logs under Ava and Brant, to kindle the illusion the network wanted. But he couldn't do that while Ava's attention was on *him*.

And, man, did he want her attention on him. He closed his eyes, letting all the feelings and mental pictures that had occupied his nights lately flood through him. It was as though she'd stained him with her essence wherever she'd touched, kissed.

She quite literally haunted him—day and night.

He pushed away from the kitchen bench, swallowing back another third of the beer as he paced. She'd invaded his life. Snuck up and taken it over. The level of cruel he'd just been to her was directly proportional to amount of hold she had over him.

And that made him nervous. Getting attached to someone had never been part of his ten year plan. Particularly *that* someone.

He set the bottle on the bench and ran his hands roughly through his hair with a grimace. He'd been brutal. Intentionally. Gnawing off the last sinews of friendship so that he would be free to manage this situation unencumbered. He couldn't think straight when Ava was near, let alone act decisively.

She hated him now. It had been written all over her flushed face as she'd let him have it with both barrels. She'd handed him the opportunity to put some distance between them on a silver platter. And he'd ripped her heart out with it.

His particular speciality.

He took a final swallow of frigid beer and relished the ache of it freezing in his gut. The pain was no less than he deserved. A sudden flash of grey eyes, bright with accusation and confused hurt, trebled the size of the rock in his gut.

Ashamed of me, Ava? He pitched the empty bottle into the trash and turned towards the hall. *Nowhere near as ashamed as I am of myself.*

CHAPTER EIGHT

'WHERE is everyone?' Brant suavely squired Ava through the restaurant doors, scanning the room for any sign of their colleagues.

She glanced at her watch. 'It's just after seven-thirty. Where are they?' She looked at the name emblazoned on the wall. Scarparolo's—right restaurant.

'Here comes Dan.' Brant said it so casually, oblivious to the effect the simple words had on Ava. She steeled herself not to turn and look.

'Maddox.'

'Arnot.' Ava knew Brant well enough now to spot his very subtle use of sarcasm as he mirrored Dan's unfriendly greeting. She turned casually and met Dan's eyes. Or would have if they'd been trained on her. He looked flustered. Distracted. He crossed to the *maître d'* and had a quick conversation. When he returned, with a black-clad waitress in tow, he addressed them both briskly, his gaze barely acknowledging her.

'I'm just heading out to the car. I forgot my phone. You two go ahead and take a seat.'

He departed, sparing only the briefest glance for her. His brown eyes were dark with anger. She sighed. Hostilities had resumed, then.

She turned her attention to the table she and Brant were being directed to. By the window, candle flickering, beautifully set.

For two.

'Uh..?' Brant looked as confused as Ava felt. Their waitress stared at him, dazzled, but remembered to slide Ava's chair out. Brant caught his lapse of manners and took over, gliding the chair in as Ava sat.

'Excuse me?' she queried, finally drawing the woman's eyes off her co-host. 'We should be part of a larger group? The AusOne booking?'

The waitress looked nonplussed for a moment, before flashing her previous perfect smile. 'One moment, I'll just check.' She drifted over to the *maître d'*. A furious whispered discussion behind a stack of menus ensued.

Brant smiled gallantly at Ava, his public face firmly in place. He took her fingers in his. 'Looks like you'll have the pleasure of my company to yourself for now. Try not to swoon.'

Ava laughed and glanced out of the window. In that instant a car turned onto the dark street, spotlighting the road ahead with its headlights. In the distance, beyond the glare, Ava thought she saw Dan in conversation with a shadowy figure on the sidewalk. It didn't look like a relaxed conversation. She frowned.

Brant raised her hand to his lips. She restrained the impulse to pull it free, conscious that there was more than one pair of speculative eyes in the restaurant. Whatever Brant's game was, he was a friend, and she owed him the courtesy of playing along in public. But later…

She spoke through the careful smile plastered on her face and tried to disentangle her hand, worrying that Dan could probably see them from his position out in the street. Not that he would care. 'Oh, please, you've had me to yourself practically all day. I swear the network must not trust me in a scene alone.'

His face lost some of its slick. 'You're doing a great job, Ava. Has no one told you that?'

She squeezed her fingers gratefully around his and lowered them decisively to the table. 'None so sincerely. Thank you, Brant.'

The puzzled waitress returned and said brightly, 'There does seem to have been an error. You're seated over on the large reserved table. Your booking was for eight p.m.' There was no blame, only confusion in her voice.

Ava frowned. 'My call sheet said seven-thirty.'

Brant's surprise mirrored hers. 'Mine, too. The call sheet never lies.'

Just then Dan walked through the door of the restaurant, phone in hand, colour high. His eyes connected with Ava's immediately, then dropped to where her fingers were still gently clutched in Brant's. She slid them free as he approached.

They followed the waitress to a table at the rear of the restaurant set for more than a dozen.

'Looks like even executives can have scheduling malfunctions,' Brant said casually. 'We're not due until eight.'

Ava's nape prickled. Good point.

'Don't let me interrupt your earlier conversation,' Dan said, deftly changing the subject. 'Pretend I'm not here.'

Oh, would that she could!

Brant looked at him, eyes narrowing. 'Actually, I was telling Ava what a great job she's doing. It seems she's been made to feel...inadequate.'

Ava studied the embroidered tablecloth furiously, but felt Dan's eyes on her.

Brant went on. 'A little more praise might be in order from the higher end of the food chain.'

Ava hadn't heard this steely tone from Brant before. Her eyes rose, but Brant's gaze was locked firmly on Dan's. Tension surged between them. Then Dan's heated focus shifted to her, pinning her like a butterfly in a museum. She immediately regretted speaking, coming out tonight at all. When would she learn?

'My apologies, Ava. You didn't strike me as someone who needed constant reinforcement.'

Desperate to move the conversation away from her, she parried, 'I don't, but I was curious as to why I'm yet to be trusted with a scene by myself.'

A tiny crease appeared between Dan's brows. 'Those decisions have nothing to do with your abilities—'

'So you say,' Brant risked from across the table.

Dan fixed him with an irritated stare. 'I do say. Let's order some drinks, shall we?'

Ava was intrigued at the by-play between the two men flanking her. It had all the hallmarks of a peeing contest. Brant had dropped all pretence and looked as if he was thriving on the chilly encounter. For his part, Dan was matching him head-on. Brown eyes locked with blue ones.

Brant looked away first. He picked up the menu, and in an instant the charmer was back. He smiled winningly at the dazzled waitress and ordered an expensive bottle of wine. Ava occupied herself with filling each of their water glasses from the carafe in front of her, used the moment to steady her hands. Though she steadfastly avoided Dan's eyes, she was conscious of them, narrowed and glancing between herself and Brant. The air was thick with unasked questions.

She discreetly peeked at her watch. A quarter to eight.

Oh, please let someone be early.

'I'm done, Bill.'

Dan tossed the early edition on the desk in front of Bill Kurtz without bothering to sit. He wasn't staying long. 'It's not working for me, and its not working for the show.'

The older man smirked, not glancing at the newspaper. He'd already seen it, then.

'Ava-ricious!' the headline called her, claiming she'd wasted no time in snaffling her pretty-boy host for herself. There was even an incriminating picture—Ava Lange and Brant Maddox in a romantic candlelit tryst.

'Give it a chance to work, Dan. We've only just started.'

Dan pressed his thumbnail into the flesh of his index finger hard, and concentrated on the dull pain. It was an old trick he'd developed when he was a kid. To manage the anger. To control it. Possibly the only practical life skill he'd taken from his relationship with his father.

'This show can succeed on its own. You've seen the dailies— it's coming up beautifully,' Dan said. 'We don't need this.'

'Everything needs a boost.'

'This is my show. My concept. We're doing this my way.'

Kurtz glared at him. 'You don't want to get yourself a reputation, Dan. Reputations are career hurdles.'

Dan snarled. 'Lucky I'm so athletic.'

There was something in Kurtz's thin smile. Something predatory that reminded him of his father. How long had Kurtz been waiting for this moment? How disappointed must he have been every time Dan had acquiesced to the network on one ludicrous demand or another. Just waiting for the time bomb that was Dan to explode.

For the first time he saw himself through Kurtz's eyes. The young gun, rising fast, rising straight towards Kurtz's job.

The older man narrowed his gaze. Mentally reviewing Dan's contract, looking for a weakness, most likely. There were none. Dan had checked.

'I had that photographer primed,' he said. 'He knew exactly what kind of a story I wanted. This—' he flicked his fingers at the paper '—is not it.'

Someone had undermined him. Someone with really bad taste in suits.

'Since when have you ever heard of paparazzi working solo?' Kurtz said.

Son of a... There'd been a second photographer. Dan had kept the first one occupied, ridden him until he'd fired off a few simple shots and departed on a mouthful of muttered abuse. But Kurtz must have known Dan would try to control the publicity stunt and he'd arranged a second snapper.

'Tell me where the value is in portraying Ava as a scheming gold-digger. What happened to your desire to link Brant with a fresh-faced innocent?'

Kurtz didn't answer.

'You don't really care how she's portrayed, do you?' Dan suddenly realised. 'As long as she's on the second page.'

'Nor should you, Dan. This is outstanding PR, and that's our primary objective.'

Dan's lip curled. 'This is not outstanding anything. It's tabloid pap. Have you forgotten that Ava's not just the face of *Urban Nature* but she's the designer? I need her to be credible.'

For the show and for her self-worth.

'That's your problem, Dan.' A distinct chill had entered Kurtz's voice. 'You seem to have lost track of where your loyalties lie. With AusOne. The network that put you where you are today.'

'There will be no further PR relating to Ava Lange and Brant Maddox.' His voice was granite.

'Not your call.' Kurtz tried to shut him down. 'You don't want to run this yourself, fine. We have specialists to take care of this kind of thing. People who've worked this industry for a lot longer than six years.'

Dan rested his palms on the edge of the desk and leaned towards the older man. Icicles could have formed off his words. 'This is my show. Nothing happens without my authorisation.'

Kurtz glared, but leaned back. 'I have a half-a-million-dollar production bill that tells me it's the network's show, Arnot.'

'And you pay me fifty percent of that to make it the best it can be. And best doesn't include discrediting the talent.'

'That's a matter of opinion.'

His fingernails bit cruelly. Dan calculated his next move, then casually spoke. 'How good would your picture look on the front page of the *Standard* with the headline "AusOne exploits female personnel", Bill?'

Kurtz surged to his feet, dragging his belly past the desk on the way up. 'Don't you threaten me, boy. Don't you dare. This network made you, and we will break you if necessary.'

Oh, just like his father.

Dan stood his ground, steel in his voice. 'I calloused up amongst the best, Kurtz. I don't break easily.' He turned for the door. 'I will not be playing this particular game. And I'll be watching production frame-by-frame to make sure no one else does.'

'You do not control what this network does!' A spray of furious spittle fell short of Dan's side of the desk. Kurtz's raised voice earned a hush in the outer office.

Dan walked to the door before turning. He forced his body to relax. There was only one coronary in the making in this room. He pinned the blustering man with his steeliest gaze. 'Do your worst, Bill. I'll be ready for you.'

He turned and walked out of the office, mentally reviewing the coming month's filming. You didn't wave a red rag at a bull and then go and sit at your comfortable desk. He'd have to keep an even closer eye on production in coming weeks. Control things from the inside. Minimise the potential for Kurtz and his cronies to go to town on Ava. He had enough contacts in the PR department to stay across whatever disasters the executive producer was probably already conceiving.

He marched past Kurtz's gaping assistant, glancing at the garish furnishings. Some days it was hard to remember why he wanted all this so badly.

Then he visualised his father, conjured feelings from twenty years ago. Never being good enough, talented enough. Being too much like his mother to bare tolerating. The liquor. The abuse. The crushing grief of a parentless boy; one parent who abandoned him literally, and one who abandoned him emotionally. When he wasn't thrashing the living daylights out of him.

Until eight in the morning, when Mitchell Arnot suited up and went out into the public world. Popular, respected, adored by all. The town rep for Eyes-on-the-Street, for crying out loud. There was only one other living person in all of Flynn's Beach who'd had any clue what kind of a monster his father turned into behind closed doors.

James Lange.

The man Dan respected above all others. The man he'd shared his fear with. The man who had taken him in. The man who, eventually, had asked him to go.

The man whose only daughter Dan was helping to screw over.

The innocent lift button bore the brunt of Dan's fury. At Kurtz. At his father. But above all at himself.

He rubbed his eyes, breathing slowly. He couldn't tell her. She'd never forgive him if she found out he'd been any part of it.

But how would she? If he stopped now.

How would she?

'Ugh, this is awful,' Brant murmured in Ava's ear, when they paused for a moment between appearances. 'If not for the intravenous latte I'd be desolate.'

As publicity exercises went, this was one of the network's better ideas. Ava felt a thousand times more comfortable here, amongst her friends the plants, than at last week's shopping mall debacle. Or the inner city appearance before that.

Bad enough to have to endure the claustrophobic crush of shoppers pressing in on them to see exactly what celebrity *du jour* the mall was offering. Bad enough that some grunted and walked away when they saw it was just the cast of a new lifestyle programme. But to spend the entire day under fluorescent lights smiling and waving, without one single breath of fresh air all day… Intolerable.

Today, in the dappled light of a leafy boutique garden centre, Ava stood elbow-deep in potting mix, demonstrating to two dozen wealthy would-be horticulturists how to re-pot a rootbound fern. The smell of the earth, the feel of the living roots, the waft of the fragrance rich air. And this time the audience had a genuine interest in what she was doing and what she had to say. They were plant people.

Her people. Good people.

She laughed and tucked her face close to his, so there was

no risk of their hosts or audience overhearing. 'Tell you what, from now on you do all the malls and I'll do all the garden centres. Deal?'

'Woman, you have yourself a deal. Sadly, I doubt the maestro over there would let us do anything independently...'

Ava followed his gaze to where Dan stood, monitoring the day's activities. Just as Ava had finally accepted that she and Brant would share just about every scene, the PR personnel had finally accepted Dan's presence at every event. He was senior to them, after all. They could hardly tell him not to come. But it was still hard to believe how hands-on he was. Did he really trust her so little in public?

How stupid did he think she was?

'God forbid we should be seen without each other,' Brant continued. 'It might cause some kind of irrevocable breach in the space-time continuum.'

That drew Ava's glance back to Brant. 'You know, one day you're going to slip up and expose yourself as quite an intelligent man.'

'Perish the thought.' He winked at her, then spun around to face his adoring public shouting flamboyantly, 'Who's next for an autograph?'

She watched him with affection. There was little question in her mind now that Brant Maddox was a far better performer than any of them knew. He had the public and the network completely fooled. He was amazing.

'Careful, Ava, you're going to give the tabloids fodder for another story, gazing at him like that.'

Her stomach dropped and she spun round. Not that she needed to. Her tingling senses had told her exactly who it was before he even spoke. Just thinking Dan's name made her sigh.

'I doubt I need to give them anything. They seem quite capable of fabricating what they need,' she said.

There'd been two more stories published about her and Brant since the restaurant debacle. Not quite as offensive as that first one, but both complete with made-up content and carefully edited images from the PR trail. She swore the photographers must have waited, without blinking, for her and Brant to share a single up-close moment. Next thing she knew they were gracing the inside pages again—although no one had invaded her privacy quite like that first time. She wondered if the network had read the riot act to the press.

'No smoke without fire, I think the tabloids would say,' he growled.

'They'd be wrong.'

Ava was tired of Dan's ever-present attention. His constant fixation on how she presented herself with Brant. Once she would have been thrilled to be the centre of his attention like this. But now it was hard enough enduring the public frenzy, without the added pressure of him monitoring her every move. Judging. If not for the steady thrum of her heart whenever he was close she'd have thought she was finally over him.

'You carry on as though Brant and I manufacture these things intentionally. The kind of press exposure I was hoping for was related to my skills. My talent. Not my love-life. Or my supposed love-life.'

'He was kissing you in the restaurant, Ava. Hard to misinterpret that.'

'It was my *hand*, Dan. Who cares about that?'

He locked eyes with her. 'We're talking about the press. All it did was whet their appetite. From that moment you two had a paparazzi price on your heads.' He ran an agitated hand through his hair. 'Just…be careful. Don't give them any more than you have to.'

She wasn't in the mood for a fight, but it seemed the fight was finding her. 'What's that supposed to mean?'

'I thought your professional reputation meant something to you.'

'It does!'

'Then take care, Ava. This isn't Flynn's Beach. You can't

wear your heart on your sleeve in this industry.' He looked furious. But he sounded concerned. 'Just...take care. That's all.'

'Here's a crazy idea,' she said, glaring at him. 'Why not stop putting Brant and me together in front of the cameras so much? Stop feeding the frenzy?'

He considered her words and visibly discarded them. 'I think you enjoy spending time with him.'

She threw up her hands in frustration. 'Yes, actually, I do. He's the best part of this whole circus. At least he understands how I'm feeling.'

'I imagine that's part of his appeal.'

'I can't speak for all womankind but, yes, it *is* nice to have an ally on this battlefield.'

He stared steadily at her. 'When did I become the enemy?'

Ava swallowed. 'You know very well when. And that was your choice.'

An age passed before he nodded. 'Then I have nothing to lose by warning you not to get too involved with Maddox.'

Outrage warred with frustration. 'I'm *not* involved with Brant. Lord, Dan, you're as bad as the tabloids.'

'The camera says otherwise.'

'Oh, please. As if *you* can tell. I had a crush on you for years and you had no idea—' She sucked the words back too late.

Smugness settled across his features, infuriating and entirely seductive. 'I had an idea, Ava. More than an idea, actually. And long before that night on the beach. I have a radar when it comes to you.'

His eyes gleamed hazelnut and she forced herself to ignore his use of the present tense. Did he seriously think that she would go from kissing him to being with Brant in a few short weeks? 'Then your radar needs recalibrating.'

For the first time in an age he laughed. Loud and genuine. Ava blinked her astonishment and her heart squeezed hard. The laugh instantly made her think of home, and warm fires and safety.

And it made her blood thicken.

She shook her head. She *had* to get a handle on these feelings. The man had made it perfectly clear he wasn't interested. Beyond their charming little experiment in the garden, of course. And, more relevant, she wasn't interested either. Daniel Arnot was too much work. Too career-driven and too complicated. She needed someone simpler in her life. Or at least someone she had a hope of understanding.

A perverse little demon raised its head. Why not? They got on well enough. Maybe attraction would grow between them? He was certainly handsome enough. She'd worked with less in the past.

'What makes you think you have the right to tell me what to do anyway? If I choose to see Brant Maddox then that's no one's business but my own.'

Silence crackled. 'Yours and the entire country.'

'If I'm damned-if-I-do/damned-if-I-don't, then I might as well enjoy the journey.'

Dan braced his feet and crossed his arms. His suspicion burned her. 'What are you saying?'

Ava looked over to where Brant was busy flirting with the women in the crowd and still signing endless autographs. *Don't do it, Ava...*

'He's a good-looking man. We get on. Besides, I don't know many people in town. So, why not?'

'Ava...'

That manipulative tone again. Just like that first day in his office. Fury simmered in her veins. 'We're spending all our time together anyway—thanks to you.'

'I just warned you—'

'That's the thing, Dan. You don't get to warn me about anything. I'm a big girl. Just because you can't see that, it doesn't mean Brant can't.' She prayed to the angels of understanding for forgiveness on that one.

Dan's nostrils flared.

'It's win-win, Dan. You get all the on-screen togetherness you want, and I get all the off-screen togetherness I crave.'

Just not with the right man.

'Until he breaks your heart,' Dan said quietly. 'A man like that won't stay interested in a woman like you for long.'

Ava froze. Did he have no survival instincts whatsoever? 'A woman *like me*?'

'You're too white bread for him, Ava. Look at the women he's dated in the past. Wild, racy, sexy women.'

She swallowed hard on the insult. Her voice was arctic when she could finally speak past the lump of pain in her throat. 'Well, I may not be sexy, but at least you finally agree I am a woman.'

She turned and marched away from the man who had so much power to hurt her, ignoring him as he called her name. Ahead of her, Brant was finishing with the autographs. She grabbed him by the sleeve with shaking hands, pulled him over to a stand of indoor palms, turned, and slammed straight into him.

'You owe me one, right?' she warned, reaching up behind his bemused face. 'I'm calling it in.'

Then she kissed him.

To his credit, he didn't flinch—just stood frozen while she plied him with her most convincing kiss on his stunned mouth. The crowd went wild behind them. To them it must have looked as if she'd had enough of Brant flirting with the women in the crowd. Her lips ground into his, and Brant recovered enough to slide his hands around behind her and pull her even closer to him. And then he kissed her back.

That got her attention.

The anger suddenly drained right out of her and she pulled away, deflated. What was she thinking?

'I don't know what we're doing,' Brant murmured against her ear, panting slightly, 'but I thought you'd want it to look good.'

'Let 'em talk about *that* in tomorrow's paper,' she ground out bitterly, glancing over to where Dan had been standing.

He was gone.

'Ava, honey, are you crying?' Brant shifted slightly so he was between her and the rapt crowd, providing a little privacy. He stroked her hair from her face.

'No...' She swiped at her eyes, dragging dirt across her nose. She glanced at the exit gate swinging open. Brant's gaze followed hers. 'No.'

CHAPTER NINE

BRANT'S face was serious as he entered the Winnebago. 'For what's about to happen, I'm truly sorry.'

That was all the warning Ava got as a whirlwind shoved past him to invade the sanctuary of her office trailer. Brant locked the door firmly behind him as the black-clad, pale-skinned woman came to a halt a few feet in front of where Ava sat, bemused, behind her drafting table.

She glanced nervously from Brant to the heavily made-up woman. The other woman glared, uncomfortable and angry, but did not speak.

Brant finally found speech. 'Ava, this is Cadence, my—'

'His girlfriend!' The woman jerked her thumb in Brant's direction, and Ava knew immediately that Cadence was much angrier with him than she was with her.

And why.

Cadence was young and slim—that much fitted Brant perfectly—but there it ended. She had dark red hair piled messily on her head, an ancient, torn rock band T-shirt, a long layered black skirt, Doc Marten boots, full Goth make-up, and at least a dozen piercings that Ava could see.

Probably a dozen more she couldn't.

Brant's girlfriend? This woman? Self-preservation kept her silent. She moved out from behind her desk and extended her hand respectfully, testing the waters. 'Nice to meet you, Cadence.'

Cadence blinked twice, then pushed out long fingers tipped with black nail varnish. No, not black, Ava noticed as she shook the death-pale hand. It was darkest red, like Cadence's hair. Snug PVC wrist gloves fitted over elegant wrists and were laced back past her elbow. The work on the gloves was stunning.

'They're gorgeous!' Ava said, one hundred percent sincere, touching the sensual material lightly.

Cadence glared at her a moment longer, then thrust the other one out for Ava to compare.

'She designed them herself,' Brant piped up from his corner. Peacemaking, no doubt, but Ava could still hear the pride in his voice. She looked again at the young woman before her, still glowering unhappily. Bull by the horns time.

'You've come about yesterday?'

Cadence didn't answer, but her lips tightened. Brant flapped around uselessly in the background. This wasn't some casual, recent thing, Ava realised, reading the body language between the two of them. How long had they…? Oh.

Oh!

Time to fess up. 'Yesterday was my fault, Cadence. Brant had nothing to do with it.'

'That's not exactly how he tells it.' Blue, blue eyes didn't waver, blazing out at Ava from a thick smudge of charcoal.

Ava lifted her hands helplessly. 'He owed me one. And he's a good actor.' She saw uncertainty flash across Cadence's face. 'And a really good friend.'

That did it. Cadence's blue eyes blinked furiously. Ava yanked some blotting paper from her table and thrust it urgently at Cadence. 'Don't—you'll wreck your make-up.'

Cadence took it gratefully and carefully folded an edge against her eyelid to absorb the tears. 'Are you kidding? Goths kill for that look.'

Brant relaxed visibly, but didn't leave his post as guardian of the door. Ava glared at him with an open question in her eyes. What had he been thinking, telling her about the kiss?

He shrugged and said, 'I tell her everything.'

Cadence sniffed. 'I find out everything. It's in his best interests to tell me first.'

Ava smiled, and guilt nibbled at her. She'd kissed Brant selfishly, with no thought for who else it might affect.

'I'm so sorry. I didn't know Brant had a girlfriend.' This was to both of them.

'You wouldn't. I'm the Anne Frank of the television world—hidden away in the attic of anonymity.' Cadence had mopped up the worst of her tears and blew out a steadying breath. 'I don't really fit the mould.'

Ava glanced at the anxiety marring Brant's handsome face. 'How long have you two been together?' she asked.

'Since high-school.'

Years? 'But all the other—' She cut herself off. Too late.

Cadence waved her concern away. 'Women? Go ahead, say it. It's not like I don't know about them.'

'Props,' Brant clarified from his corner. 'Or a smokescreen, more rightly. It's a network thing. Keeps people guessing. Makes it easier on Cadey.'

Ava found that hard to believe, and looked at the younger woman sceptically.

'He thinks he's protecting me.' Cadence spoke with such a mix of pride, fury and frustration, Ava knew their feelings for each other ran deep. Very deep.

A nasty little green-eyed monster reared its head. When would she meet someone to defend *her* that loyally?

'But he hadn't kissed any of them,' Cadence went on. 'Until yesterday.'

A small groan escaped her. Some friend. She'd really messed things up for Brant. 'That was me, Cadence, I swear. I...um... Well, I used him to make a point, actually. I'm so sorry.' The last bit she directed straight to Brant. He shrugged, and it saddened Ava how blasé he'd become about being used by other people.

Cadence's barked snort contrasted wildly with her sombre appearance. 'That would be a nice piece of karma, then! Who were you trying to get back at?'

Heat roared up Ava's neck.

'That's Ava's business, Cadence.' Brant spoke in a way Ava had never heard, and Cadence dropped her eyes. She knew immediately who truly wore the pants in this relationship. Never mind startling appearances to the contrary.

'Right. Sorry…' Cadence trailed off awkwardly.

Ava chewed her lip. It was fair penance, after all. She had some damage to undo. She sighed and spilled the beans. 'Dan Arnot.'

The avenging angel in front of her nearly squealed, completely intrigued. 'Maverick? Really?'

'Maverick?'

'Oh, that's what I call him. The top gun in the industry and all that. Good looking. Cocky. Danger zone. You know…'

As nicknames went, it was strangely apt. Dan had always been so fearless as a younger man. Did he still have that quality now that he was older? Enough to get a nickname like that? How had she missed it? Her heart squeezed again. She was getting used to the sensation.

'Anyway,' she fumbled on, clearing her throat, 'the kiss wasn't about Brant. He was just the nearest handy male. An innocent bystander.'

'Innocent?' Cadence snorted. 'Yeah, I'm sure he didn't enjoy a second of it.'

Awkward silence descended. Ava felt some heat rising. Saw it echoed in Brant's face. Time for a subject change. 'So, you design fashion?'

Cadence shrugged. 'Goth stuff, mostly. Punk.' Her eyes strayed to Ava's shambolic workbench. 'I guess we have something in common. Designing.'

'I guess so. Want to see?'

The two women pored over Ava's most recent design, and

she showed Cadence how she worked in layers from the bare schematics of the space she was renovating.

'I watch all the shows,' Cadence murmured, not looking at her. 'I really like what you do. And how you present. Can't say I'm crazy about how you and Brant come across…' Ava looked at her about to apologise again. Cadence waved her concern away with a quick flash of the PVC gloves. 'No, I get it. All must bow down before the mighty ratings god. No wonder they've been thrusting you guys together so much.'

Ava blinked. She knew her rapport with Brant was good for the show, but it hadn't dawned on her that it was so…engineered. She spoke the word aloud.

'Right. Exactly. I know it's not real, my family knows, our friends know—sort of. But, still, it's hard to watch.'

She nodded, empathising completely. It was hard enough hiding her feelings about Dan from Dan himself. She couldn't imagine how hard it would be keeping a secret like this from the whole country.

Or being deemed sub-standard just for being yourself.

The thought must have filled the air, because suddenly Brant moved away from his station by the door and came to stand right behind Cadence. She fitted perfectly under his chin as his arms came around her. He rested it lightly on her head and tucked her into him.

As odd a pair as they made, it was achingly sweet. And perfectly right. Brant looked like a different man when he was with the love of his life. And Cadence quite obviously was.

She felt more than a pang of jealousy. Not for Brant, but for the love.

'What if I *had* kissed him?' curiosity made her ask. 'With intent, I mean? What would you have done?'

Cadence didn't hesitate. 'I would have fought for him.'

Looking at the determination in the young woman's eyes, she didn't doubt it for a second.

Cadence stared at her for a moment, her mind ticking away

behind expressive blue eyes. 'Can I ask a favour?' she suddenly said, full of determination.

Ava nodded and laughed. 'After yesterday, you can ask for a few!'

'No, just one. It's a big one. Chalk this up under "Better-the-devil-you-know", but…would you continue to hang out with Brant? I'd feel much better knowing it's you he's with than some of those other…*women* the network finds.' The way she spat the word spoke volumes about exactly what Cadence thought the women really were.

Ava considered quickly. She hadn't lied when she'd said she enjoyed Brant's company, and now she knew he was happily in love with Cadence any vestige of concern that he might form an attachment to her thoroughly evaporated. And it wasn't as though Ava had her own relationship to protect.

'I'd be happy to, Cadence.' She looked at Brant, too. 'Until my contract's finished.'

'Thank you.' Relief filled Cadence's pale-powdered face and showed Ava the young woman as she really must look beneath the layers of make-up. The slim hand she wrapped around Ava's was warm now, and unhesitant in its squeeze.

Cadence apologised for bursting into the RV, and Ava laughed her concern away. Then Brant nudged Cadence and pointed to his watch. They said reluctant farewells and Ava hinted that she'd be happy to tag along if the two of them ever wanted to hang out. Do a movie. Anything.

Maybe Cadence could be a good friend, despite their disastrous start. And Ava sorely needed friends here in the city. Cadence led the way out of the RV and marched off to the right. Brant shot Ava a grateful glance over his shoulder as he started to turn left.

The manoeuvre hit her in the solar plexus. How hard for them to constantly need to pretend the other didn't exist.

'Brant?' Her soft voice stilled him. He turned his handsome face to her. 'She's perfect for you.' It wasn't lip service. Ava could no longer remember the type of woman she'd thought was right for Brant. Only crazy, gothic Cadence.

His heartbreaking smile was full of love. 'I know.'

Ava sighed as the door closed behind them and they went their separate ways. There went a woman who had every reason in the world to give up on her love and crawl into a hiding place to die. But, no, she stayed, and worked hard behind the scenes to reinforce her relationship. And she fought for her man.

There was a lesson in that.

Something had changed between Ava and Maddox. Dan couldn't quite define it, but there was a level of comfortableness that hadn't been there before. He didn't know where it was coming from, but he knew that he absolutely did *not* want Ava getting comfortable with Maddox.

He didn't want her doing anything with Maddox.

Too late for that, a dark little voice reminded him. The mental image of Ava kissing the vapid pretty boy, his hands sliding down over her body, was seared into Dan's mind.

He swore.

He wasn't having much luck keeping her on the safe side of the line he'd drawn in the sand. If she wasn't stumbling over it herself, then he was manufacturing unconscious ways to drag her over. And what did it say about him that he'd been willing to exploit Ava to give the network its way.

Not very much.

Another image of Maddox bending to Ava, kissing her enthusiastically, flashed through his head. It only served to fire him up more.

Dan knew he'd handled that one badly—had virtually pushed Ava into Maddox's arms yesterday. He remembered too late how prone she'd always been to doing the exact opposite of what she wanted if it happened to be what *he* didn't want. Or her brother or her father. Or anyone who was telling her what to do.

So much for having grown up!

Flash. Ava's lips on Maddox's in the moments before Dan had walked away in pained disgust. Then—*flash*—the feel of Ava's lips on his own. Pliant. So addictive. So unquestionably adult.

Get a grip.

Dan shook his head as he waited for the lift to take him to the rooftop they were working on this week. Not a true roof, more of a giant outdoor space about halfway up a thirty-storey high-rise. When they'd first scoped out this site it had been a bare tiled space with a few tip-burned potted palms abused as a convenient ashtray by smokers in any of the three hundred offices on nearby floors. Today it was a half-finished tranquillity garden, filled with wind-tolerant species suited to an exposed location this close to the coast.

It was going to make magnificent television.

His eyes found Ava the second he emerged onto the set. She was talking through some design features with one of her offsiders, Shannon. He knew the moment she sensed him by the sudden stiffness of her back and the way her fists curled into little balls. Her assistant noticed as well, and glanced around to see what had caused it.

'Hey, Mr Arnot,' Shannon called, oblivious to any undercurrents.

He returned her greeting casually and walked straight by, without acknowledging Ava. It took some doing when he really wanted to grab her and drag her away somewhere private to talk. More than talk. But she didn't so much as glance at him, so he kept walking, furiously trying to fabricate some errand on the far side of the set to justify arriving there.

Maddox's knowing eyes met his halfway across the rooftop. Dan's narrowed. What the hell was he looking so smug about? Instantly his hackles rose. It was bad enough imagining those slimy hands all over Ava's perfect flesh without having to endure his gloating, too. He hadn't realised how much pleasure he'd got from knowing he'd tasted Ava, touched her, felt her body against his…while she hadn't shared any of that with Maddox.

Now that the playing field was more even, he didn't like it one bit.

His smile was tight as he reached the First Assistant Director on the far side of the set and asked a few vaguely salient questions about the day's shoot. Not that he heard a word of the answer. His focus was across the roof with Ava. She'd finished her dealings with Shannon and was scanning the crowded rooftop. Her eyes landed on Maddox.

The smile she gave the man made Dan's abs tighten.

He forced his eyes down, to maintain the illusion that he was listening to the AD. When he looked back, it was in time to see Ava move up next to Maddox and rest her hand lightly on his arm, laughing easily at something he said. It killed him that Maddox could inspire such warmth in Ava and all *he* inspired was pain. His foot ground into the gravel that had just been introduced to the rooftop.

A moment later his distinctive ringtone pealed out across the roof, drawing all eyes, including Ava's. He dragged his focus away and snapped his mobile open on a curse.

He was in no mood for anything more challenging than his stock update.

Kurtz started in with one of his monologues. The only blessing was that it didn't require Dan to listen particularly hard. He glanced over at Ava, where she was joking around with Maddox as they prepared the next shot set-up. Kurtz droned on about ratings and broadcast numbers.

'Anyway, I wanted to pass on the good news personally.' The unusual tone in Kurtz's voice brought Dan's attention back to the phone call. 'It's official. *Urban Nature* is a nominee for an Australian Television Award. Best New Lifestyle Programme.'

Dan sucked in his breath.

'The first time a programme has been nominated this early into its first season—'

'This is its second season, don't forget,' Dan said, irritated that they could so easily overlook a whole season of television. A year of his life.

'Everyone has forgotten the first season, Dan. It's *this* season they're all talking about. The whole Ava/Maddox thing is working a charm, as is our new no-bull format.'

Our... Dan knew how many meetings it had taken to lock down a bit of verity in television. AusOne had haemorrhaged steel filings over the simple idea of showing the construction as it truly was. The real size of the team. The actual amount of work. The true price tag.

'The odds are in our favour, Dan. But the network is keen to capitalise on the exposure.'

'In what way?' Dan's neck hairs prickled. They were already running a PR extravaganza on the side—what more could they expect?

'The short PR pieces have been great, but we're looking for something longer. More substantial. In-depth. We're thinking print. Feature article. A-day-in-the-life type thing.'

Dan cringed. How had someone whose taste was so firmly implanted up their butt risen so high in AusOne's ranks? His teeth ground together. 'And I assume you want me to broker this?'

'Not in a million years, sunshine. You had your chance. Although I'd have thought you'd be all over this, Dan—a chance to get a nice high-profile paperweight for your desk. Runs on the board. Generate some real interest in the public.'

The network weren't yet aware of the very real, very public kiss Ava and Maddox had shared the day before. Kurtz's PR stooge had been inside on the phone when Maddox and Ava had tangled tongues. There'd only been one photographer there, but Dan's investigations had revealed he was a stringer for a number of magazines. If the photo appeared in one, they could guarantee real interest brewing in the public.

The network would be delighted.

They'd be the only ones.

Now they wanted a full-on journo to be given access to Ava. Potentially the sort who could take a kiss like that and turn it into something far more sordid. Dan knew any number of that calibre. And a few who weren't.

An idea began forming.

'Let me know when they're coming.' He signed off, any pleasure about the unprecedented award nomination floundering beneath his concern about the feature article.

He could try and swing it to Tannon or Larks, both good journalists from competing papers and tending towards the more moderate side of their business. One of their papers was likely to be thrown the exclusive. If he could swing it, either of those writers might actually stay focussed on the show rather than the private life of its hosts.

Lives.

Dan swore. Even he was linking Maddox and Ava together in his mind now.

It was worth a shot. It was the only way he could think of to keep things from escalating. He looked through narrowed eyes to where Ava and Maddox now stood talking by the coffee station, heads dipped in some confederacy. He'd have to talk to them both. The amount of time they spent with their heads bent might alert the rawest of journos. And that was the last thing they all needed.

Dammit. What had changed between them? It was driving him crazy.

And yet a big part of him really didn't want to know the answer.

'Are you serious?'

Brant's voice rose an entire octave. He scooped Ava up in a massive bear hug and spun her round while the faces all around them broke into big smiles and murmurs of congratulation. She clung on for dear life, laughing.

'An ATA this early in a season is an Australian first,' Dan

said. 'We can all be really proud. More than other programmes, this one truly is a team effort.'

Ava glanced at Dan. It felt good to be smiling at him again. Meeting Cadence had put a few things in perspective. It wasn't his fault he didn't have feelings for her, would never look at her like Brant looked at Cadence. Or think of Ava the way she thought of him. But she had no idea where to start with putting things right.

This news provided exactly the sort of introduction she needed.

'We'll be hosting a journalist on set in a few days,' he continued, 'for some pre-award coverage. There's interest in a full story on the show and its inception.'

Not entirely true, but it would be if he got his way. He released the gathered crew for a spontaneous coffee break and retreated to examine the latest part of the garden. Ava grabbed her chance and drifted up behind him.

'Congratulations, Dan. You must be so pleased.'

He turned slowly. Appraised her with those bottomless brown eyes. Her heart did its familiar squeeze thing.

'When the network's happy, I'm happy,' he said.

'You don't look all that happy.' As openings went, it wasn't bad.

He considered her, his eyes dark. 'In some ways I'd rather we'd got there the traditional way. Rather than trading so heavily on the chemistry between you and Maddox. The show has plenty of merit on its own without that.'

That mirrored Ava's own feelings almost exactly, but coming so hard on the heels of meeting Cadence, she suddenly saw the opportunity to make good on her promise to her two friends slipping away.

'Maybe the audience is responding to both? It certainly hasn't harmed anyone.'

'Hasn't it?' His dark eyes swept the set.

Could he not even look at her? She persevered, intent on trying to salvage something of their friendship. 'Give yourself a break, Dan.'

He looked at her then. Hard. 'You've changed your tune. A week ago you loathed the publicity stuff.'

Ava's essential feelings hadn't changed. But her promise to Cadence made the publicity more bearable. Gave it a purpose. 'I've come to terms with it. I know it's important to the show. To you.'

His eyes narrowed. 'Me?'

'I know how important success is to you—successes like this one. Awards and little blue numbers on a printout. If me getting on well with Brant helps that…why wouldn't you use it?'

Ava was startled by the bouquet of curses that Dan thrust at her. He pulled her further out of the way of prying ears, yanking her around behind a large ficus, and spat out a question. 'Does your perfection have no end?'

She stared at him, shocked. 'I don't mind—'

'Oh, give me a break. You don't *mind* your face being splashed all over the newspapers? Your relationship with Maddox?'

'There is no relationship.' She was tired of defending herself. But knew she only had herself to blame. This time.

'Your *thing* with Maddox, then.'

Exasperation made her short. 'It's not a thing, Dan…'

'Oh? You go around kissing just anyone, then? Oh wait, yeah—I guess you do. You kissed me not so long ago. Should I be putting an alert out to all the male members of the crew?'

Mortification streaked through her. Heat raced into her cheeks. 'That was different.'

'Why? Because you have some latent childhood crush thing going on? Time to get over that, isn't it, Ava?'

The heat fled. 'Don't! Don't ridicule what I felt.' *Feel.* Her voice broke slightly.

Dan sighed and tugged exasperated hands through his hair. 'You should be furious with me, Ava. I've treated you appallingly, and yet you stand here trying to make me feel better about what I've done. Why is that?'

There was no way she could answer that question honestly.

Not now. 'Because you're my friend, Dan. And friends look out for each other.'

'Oh, grow a spine, Ava. If you're going to make it in this industry you can't let people walk all over you like this.'

Hurt gnawed through her chest cavity, aiming for her heart. 'That's what you don't get about me, Dan. I have no interest in making it in this industry. And I don't *let* anyone walk over me.' At Dan's sceptical expression, she barrelled on. 'I'm going along with this charade because it helps someone I care about— despite not particularly liking the man you've turned into. You were part of my family growing up and you filled an important place in my life.' She dropped her voice. 'And so if it helps you to have me seen in public with Brant, and it helps him to be seen with me, and it doesn't hurt me…' *terminally* '…then why not? That's what friends do for each other, Dan. Or have you been alone so long you've forgotten the concept of loyalty?'

Pain, confusion and anger all warred at once in his hard brown eyes. Ava's heart thumped high in her throat, squeezing around the icy lump that spread steadily in her chest. 'If there's something you need and it's in my power to do it, then I will.'

'Why, Ava?' It was a half-whisper.

Because I love you.

'Because that's who I am, Dan. I may not win any prizes for street smarts, or survive very long in this piranha pool of an industry, but I will at least still be me. And I happen to like who I am.' She straightened her shoulders and forced the words out before turning back to her work. 'Even if you don't.'

CHAPTER TEN

SINCE the day she'd moved in, Dan had virtually disappeared. Ava had all the privacy she wanted and more. It had been days since she'd seen him for longer than a few seconds. Which meant she was stupid not to have expected the knocking at her front door. She answered it.

'Are you insane?' Her brother stood on her doorstep, pressing a copy of a gossip magazine under her nose.

Hi, Sis. Good to see you. 'It's not quite how it looks, Steve.'

'Oh? You *don't* have your tongue down Maddox's throat?'

She sighed, knowing she'd brought this one on herself, and stood clear to let him into the guesthouse. 'It was just a kiss. It didn't mean anything.'

'Just a kiss in front of a hundred people? On every magazine stand in the country?'

'Okay, not my finest moment.'

Steve must have seen the anguish on her face because he eased off. 'Maddox, Ava? *Maddox?*'

'What does everyone have against Brant? He's been nothing but lovely to me.'

Steve snorted and flopped onto the sofa. 'He's trying to get in your pants. It's in his best interests to be lovely.'

'He is not, Steve. Don't be so crude.'

The look Steve gave her spoke volumes. 'Oh, so *you* were kissing *him* in this photo, yes?'

Yes, actually. 'Lord, if its not you, it's Dan,' she said. 'What do you both have against Brant?'

'Maddox is bad news. He's constantly in the papers with his latest piece of—'

'That's not the man that I see every day at work.'

'It wouldn't be, would it? You're in his sights,' Steve said.

Hashing this out wasn't going to undo Steve's prejudice. She changed tack. 'How's Dad? Has he seen this?'

'No. But he will eventually. Someone will show him.'

So much fall-out from one stupid moment of thoughtlessness. It didn't matter whether it was real or not. In fact her father would be just as mortified to know that she'd used Brant to score points. That was not the daughter he'd raised.

'Can you explain?' she pleaded. 'When you go home this afternoon? Tell him it's not what it seems?'

Steve shook his head. 'I'm not going back until tomorrow. I'm heading out with Dan tonight.'

It was irrational to feel a jealous pang at that news. Just like when they were younger, and he'd got to hang out with Dan all the time and she hadn't. Maybe Dan was right? Maybe she hadn't matured emotionally at all. 'Tomorrow, then? Will you explain to Dad?'

'You want me to tell him that you've been photographed swapping saliva with a man you're *not* involved with?'

Ava rubbed her aching temples. How had this all got so complicated? 'Please just tell him…that I'm losing my way. Six months is such a long time, but I'm doing the best I can.'

Steve pulled himself to his feet and crossed to the sofa, then dropped next to her and wrapped a big-brother arm around her. She sagged into his familiar warmth. Some of her anxiety soaked away. 'Things are…complicated. I should have known they would be,' she said.

She could almost hear Steve's eyes narrow to slits with his next words. 'Is this complication Dan-related?' he asked, dangerously neutral.

She straightened carefully. 'Why would you say that?'

'Come on, Ava. I was there. I saw how you felt about him.'

Ava pointed at the magazine on the coffee table. 'That photo is doing the rounds and you've somehow drawn a connection to Dan?'

'It may surprise you to know that I believe you when you say there was nothing to that kiss with Maddox.'

Relief washed through her. 'You do?'

'But that's not you, Ava.' Shame sliced through her. 'Something had to be driving you to those lengths. It doesn't take a genius to eventually arrive at Dan's doorstep. You've always done stupid things when he's around.'

Ava took a deep breath. She glanced at the bed just a few metres away, where Dan might have made love to his best mate's little sister. The one he was supposed to be watching out for. She could make things really difficult for him with just a few sentences.

'Dan's not the problem, Steve.' *Oh, such lies.* 'I'll just be happy when this contract is over and I can go back to being me.'

'You're still you, kiddo.' He glanced at the magazine and cleared his throat. 'At least most of the time. Just don't let them suck all the goodness out of you.' Such displays of emotion were rare in her brother, and he didn't look entirely comfortable. He nudged her sideways. 'I'd hate to have to assume the role of the good one in the family.'

Ava laughed. 'I'd have to fall much further from grace for that to happen.'

The teasing continued for the next hour, and Ava let herself enjoy having family with her. Unconditional love. They chatted and joked over a constant supply of fresh coffee.

'What are you guys doing tonight?' she eventually asked.

'Dan's got some club in mind. The waitresses serve food off their bellies.'

Her eyes shot wide. She had a sudden flash of Dan's tongue circling a chilli mussel out of a delicate belly button.

'Kidding. Don't look so horrified—jeez. We'll probably hit the waterfront, catch up.' He shrugged. 'Guy stuff.'

Guy stuff. That encompassed a lot, and none of it wholesome. Suddenly the nightclub didn't seem so unlikely.

It was nearly midnight when Ava returned from her movie with Cadence. What an unexpected delight to find someone willing to indulge her passion for classic cinema. She'd managed to put the disasters of the past month well and truly behind her as she fell enthusiastically into a rich European saga of love, betrayal and intrigue. It had been a blessed three hours of pure escapism. Plus trailers.

And some good old-fashioned girl time with her unconventional new friend.

Her answering machine was flashing when she walked in from the ferry. She kicked off her shoes and tossed her handbag onto the sofa as the first message started to play. Thirty seconds later she was sprinting, barefoot, for Dan's front door.

Please, let them be home.

Her father's voice had been full of concern, desperate to get in touch with Steve. James Lange didn't usually *do* desperate. She rang the doorbell twice, then, impatient, followed it up with a brisk knock. There was not a sound inside. She glanced at her watch. Would they be home by now? *Damn!*

She turned to sprint back to her place and then spun round, eyes wide, as a light came on in the imposing portico.

'Ava?'

She rushed past Dan into his house. She could apologise for her rudeness later. 'Where's Steve?'

'Gone.'

That stopped her in her tracks. 'Gone where?' Panic rose in her voice.

'To Flynn's Beach. He got a text message from your father.'

Relief flooded through her. Steve was already on his way home. 'Oh, good. I got this call…' Her hands started to shake.

Dan steered her to the tall leather stools lining a granite-topped breakfast bar. 'Not sure what was going on, but Dad sounded urgent. He never sounds urgent.'

Her heart was thumping a tattoo. Ava told herself it was because of her fright, and not because Dan was standing before her in nothing but a pair of silk boxer shorts. She glanced down the darkened hall to where light spilled from a doorway. She finally noticed his messed-up hair and her hand shot to her mouth.

'Oh, you were sleeping!'

A slight flush stained his jawline. 'Not exactly.'

She gasped as understanding flooded in. What had he done? Hit his little black book right after waving Steve off? 'You have someone here. I'll go...' She stumbled off the stool towards the front door.

He stopped her with two hard hands on her shoulders. 'I was in bed—alone—but not yet asleep. Relax, Ava. You've interrupted nothing important.'

Oh. Then why did he look so distracted?

'Weren't you supposed to be having dinner off a stripper or something?'

His harsh laugh barked through the silence as he moved into the kitchen. The powerful topography of his back shifted as he reached into an overhead cupboard for coffee. Ava studied the nearby microwave intently.

'That'll be your brother's fertile imagination at work, then!' he said. 'We went for a beer, and then he got your dad's message. He left straight away. Lucky he'd only had the one.'

'Oh.' She nibbled her lip. 'I wonder what happened.'

'Something about his stud stallion and an altercation with a *post-n-rail* fence.'

'Oh, no—Vasse. Steve loves that animal!'

'He treated the call with the urgency it obviously deserved. I dropped him at his car and he took off immediately. He left you a message on your machine.'

She blushed. 'I didn't stick around to hear the second message.'

They fell into silence and, with crisis averted, Ava was suddenly embarrassed by her dramatic arrival and conscious of everything that had gone on between them earlier in the week.

And that he was near naked.

She cleared her throat and slid off the stool until her toes touched the cool slate floor. 'I'm sorry I pushed my way in here. I'll let you get to bed.'

'Ava, wait.'

She paused midway across the room, dreading what was coming next.

'I owe you an apology,' he said.

Her face snapped up and her breath hitched. Not what she was expecting!

He watched her warily from behind the kitchen bench, a thousand uncomfortable miles away. 'What I said yesterday. It was unnecessary and rude. And I'm sorry.'

Apologies clearly didn't come naturally to him. Not the new Dan. 'Which part?' she asked.

He grimaced. 'All of it, but particularly about what you and Maddox have going. It's none of my business. I was just... concerned.'

Ava blinked cautiously, then returned slowly to her stool. The sight of his naked torso in the kitchen had her imagining that the rest of him was naked too. Naked and making her coffee. Suddenly she couldn't think of a thing to say.

Or how to speak.

He filled two mugs with piping hot water from an elegant spout fixed to the wall. He stirred one sugar into hers, then slid it over to her, black.

'Hope you don't mind instant.'

She was too amazed that he'd remembered how she liked her coffee to care. The last coffee he'd made her had been nearly a decade ago.

'I'll be right back.' He padded up the darkened hallway.

She took a deep, steadying breath, then pulled the aromatic

brew towards her. Her cold hands shook slightly from the fright of the past ten minutes. She warmed them on the expensive ceramic mug.

Dan returned a moment later, a navy blue robe providing considerably more modesty. It was still creased from where it had been folded, and a price tag swung off the collar. Ava stepped towards him and reached her hand around behind his neck.

He froze on the spot. His eyes fluttered shut.

She broke the tag free and stepped away, handing it to him. 'You don't get around in this much, then?'

His smile was sheepish. His blush endearing. 'I'm not used to putting more clothes *on* when there's a woman in the house.'

I'll bet. Just another reminder of the world he now mixed in. And how she didn't fit.

With less hard flesh on display, she could think again. She didn't want to be angry with him. He was her friend—someone she wanted to like and respect. There were things he'd done that she wasn't crazy about, but it was hardly his fault that she couldn't think straight when he was around. That he drove her to do stupid things.

Like kissing Brant.

'We're not involved. Brant and I,' she said on a rush. Dan raised a single expressive eyebrow. She took a deep breath and raised her chin. 'You made me angry. That's why I kissed him.'

'It's none of my business.'

Lord, what was worse? His infuriating excessive interest in what she was doing, and with whom, or this new lifeless disinterest.

'You were judging me based on nothing but the speculation of a bunch of tabloid reporters. It made me mad,' she said.

'And do you always express your anger in such physical terms?'

Ava blushed. 'The only person I owe that explanation to is Brant. He was most immediately affected.'

'Oh, I saw how affected he was.'

His gaze strayed down to her bare feet, twisting awkwardly on the footplate of her stool. Not wanting to show how nervous he was making her, Ava consciously arched them, elongating her ankle where a delicate silver anklet rested. His eyes snapped back to hers, flaring briefly.

'Brant is not the man you think he is,' she risked.

Dan's jaw clenched. 'I'm fairly sure we've covered this already.'

'I just want you to understand…'

'Why is it so important that I understand?'

There were a number of answers to that, and none of them good. The nervous breath Ava blew out lifted her fringe. 'Because he's a good person. And he's being unfairly judged. Having had a taste of assassination by media myself, I can empathise.'

His eyes flashed and darkened, and she knew that was too low a blow. It was hardly Dan's fault that the media were suddenly crucifying her.

'That doesn't answer my question,' he said. 'Why is it so important to you that *I* understand?'

'I'm trying to explain…about Brant.'

He surged to his feet. 'I'm so sick of talking about Brant bloody Maddox. Everything revolves around him. He isn't even here and he's dominating the conversation.'

Ava let her mouth snap shut, realising at last that she was on dangerous ground. She glanced at the door and considered her escape. He moved into her line of sight, blocking her exit.

'Too late, Ava. You wanted to know what happens when I get mad? Well, you're about to find out.'

He closed the space between them in one fluid movement, stepping effortlessly between their stools. One arm slid around her while the other burrowed into her thick hair to hold her face still. Then he hauled her towards him. His lips pressed into hers, angled and possessive and his tongue charmed its way inside her mouth. Ava stole a lungful of air in the split second that he realigned his mouth to fit his lips more perfectly against hers.

The oxygen did little to ease the spinning of her mind, and her protest came out more of a moan than a squeak. She battled the carnal desire to lean into him, fighting the seduction of his personal scent until finally he noticed. The bruising pressure of his lips instantly eased. His mouth brushed rather than consumed. The iron bars of his arms relaxed their hold and his kisses gently nipped where only moments ago they'd crushed so violently.

'Ava.' It was more a breath than a word. He lifted his head, gazing through molten eyes, his voice thick and hoarse. 'I can't stand knowing that my kiss wasn't the last one on your lips.' Large hands framed her face.

A single kiss. Another.

Soft, now, and seductive. Hands stroking. Ava felt her tension melting. Wait—she was still angry with him. Wasn't she? She held firm. His lips grazed back and forth over hers. Tempting. Healing. Erasing any memory of the harsh treatment of moments ago. He bit gently at the fullness of her lower lip. Tasting and exploring.

Until she burned to kiss him.

Muscles deep inside her tightened and her Judas body swayed towards his. The smell of him seduced her, eddying around her as she fought the desire to taste him all over again.

His lips stopped moving against hers. He didn't pull away, but let bare millimetres open up between his stilled lips and her pulsing ones, offering her the next move. Giving her the choice.

She took it.

It was nothing like their fist kiss. And everything like it. She pressed herself into Dan's hard warmth, increasing the contact of her lips on his. It was easy—easy and natural—to open her mouth to fit better over his. To let her tongue steal out and engage his in a flirty dance. The moment she pressed her lips to his all the tension flowed out of him. As if he'd been expecting her to push him away. Those silk-covered arms, all muscle and warmth, dropped away, leaving just their mouths clinging together.

He slid his palms up her thighs, ruching her dress higher, then nudged her knees apart with his hips. Ava gasped at the startling intimacy of the move, at his boldness and what it meant, but she didn't clench them shut. Without taking his mouth from hers, he stepped further between them, and then gently closed her knees against his thighs, trapping him inside her grip. Then he tangled his fingers into her hair.

She tore her mouth from his and sucked in a deep breath in the brief seconds before Dan reclaimed her. It was no prelude to something more racy. He just wanted to be closer. *To her.* Her heart tumbled, lost, into her love for him as their kisses burned on.

Her voice was breathless when she finally lifted her head, tempering the flames with gentle humour. 'Wow. What do you do when you get mad with Steve?'

She hadn't meant to put the brakes on entirely, but his burst of laughter took care of that. He held his position between her thighs, but let his kisses drop away until the only part of him moving were his magic hands, stroking through her thick hair.

'I didn't mean any of the things I said,' he whispered, hot breath chasing across her skin. A shiver of delight followed every word. Just as well she was already sitting, because her knees went completely to liquid. 'You have to know that's not how I really think of you.'

He kissed her eyelid. Her earlobe. She whimpered at the sensation.

'You think of me as a little sister,' a breathless, sexy voice said. Lord, was that her?

He smiled and pressed closer to her body. 'Yes, because this is exactly how the average brother and sister spend their free evenings.'

She couldn't laugh when his answer meant so much.

He took pity on her, pushing her hair clear to stare intently into her grey depths. 'Ava, I stopped thinking of you of a kid the moment you walked into my office.'

'But…'

'I was lying to myself. Using that old excuse to keep some distance between us. I didn't want to get involved.'

His use of the past tense was all that kept her in her seat. 'Why?'

'Because I made a promise a long time ago. Not to hurt you. And I thought not getting involved was the easiest way to do that. But all I've done since then is cause you pain.'

'Who…?'

He stared at her long and hard. 'Your father.'

She straightened. 'My father? When? You haven't spoken to him for—'

'Nine years.'

'He warned you off me way back then?'

Dan kissed the confused creases she could suddenly feel in her brow. 'He saw the writing on the wall. Knew that you weren't getting over your…thing…for me. He asked me to take more care.'

Oh, he didn't! Heat flared in her cheeks.

'He did it because he loved you, Ava. And I left because I cared for all of you too much to stay.'

A cold dread came over her. 'You left because of me?'

'I thought it would be easier on you to make a clean break,' he said.

Easier? She'd cried herself sick for a month solid. 'But you gave up your only family. For me.' Tears sprang into her eyes.

He stroked away the tears with his thumbs. 'You were just the catalyst, Ava. I needed to leave. Needed to step out from under James's protection. It was time.'

Ava stared at him. 'Did my father ask you to go?'

Dan smiled. '"Ask" is a subjective word. Let's just say a serious talk in the kitchen one day planted the idea very firmly in my head.'

Her eyes widened. That had been her father—the hushed conversation she'd overheard. God, if only she'd stuck around to hear more of it. She never would have… *Oh, so much…*

'Why did you never call him?'

'I called once. You answered.' He traced her lips with his finger and she sighed. 'Then the next time I got your father, but he was so busy trying to convince me you were fine I knew that meant you weren't. It just made things strained between us. Either way I'd hurt you. In the end it was just easier to drop out of contact.'

Ava thought about that. 'Will you tell him that one day? So he knows? He was hurt when you left.' *Too.*

Dan looked at her, kissed her nose, her lips. His eyes held such sorrow. 'I will. If he'll speak to me.'

'Just try and stop him. He never stopped caring about you.' *Neither did his daughter.* 'So all this…hedging…was about keeping a promise you made nine years ago?'

'I owe your father a bigger debt than you can ever imagine. I figured the least I could do now was never hurt you again. Yet that's all I've done since you irritated the stuffing out of my lawyers.'

'I'm not hurting now…' She pressed her lips to his. Although she might be later. Based on their history, that was a distinct possibility.

'No?' His smile was easy.

She shook her head, side to side. Pressing her aching breasts into him. Her tongue slid so easily across his teeth, stole into his mouth to taste him, finally on her terms. She leaned into his strength and let her love steal out through that kiss. As though he would somehow taste it. She crossed her ankles behind him.

His eyes flared wide. 'Ava, you have to be sure. This is not something we can undo. Is this what you really want?'

Am I who you really want? She knew exactly where this was heading. She met his look with more control than she presently felt, and let him see the truth of her words. 'I really do, Dan.'

'This will change everything. I don't think I can go back after this.'

Back to being friends. No, that was not somewhere she wanted to go either. She stared at him, felt the blood still pumping into her aching lips, chest heaving, legs trembling.

'I don't want to be your friend,' she whispered. 'I've been your friend for a lifetime. I want to be something else.'

His next word was cautious. 'What?'

She tightened her leg-hold on him and looked him dead in the eye.

'I want to be yours.'

Warm lips murmured words close to her ear, tracing light kisses along her collarbone. Butterfly fingers stroked the flesh of her naked belly.

Ava awakened to all these things one by one.

'Ava, are you okay?'

Concerned brown eyes found her. She blinked her confusion. A husky laugh chuckled out of her. She nestled in closer to his furnace of a body. His beautiful, hard, ex-surfer's body. 'That was…'

Gravel rumbled in her ear. 'Everything I imagined.'

She tilted her head to look at him. 'You've been imagining?'

Dan laughed. 'You have no idea. Did you think you'd cornered the market on unrequited lust?' He looked down quickly.

Ah. *Not love, then.*

Ava allowed the tiny heart-bleed, even though she hadn't gone into this expecting anything more than the fulfilment of one of her own lifelong dreams. It should have been easier to swallow her disappointment after a lifetime of practice, but she got there. She stretched in his arms, lazy as only a highly satisfied woman could be.

'I've been wondering what you'd feel like,' he said. 'Since that night at the guesthouse, actually.'

'Really? So you'd been working on it? This seduction?'

'Not working. Hoping,' he said.

She eyed him seriously. What was he saying? 'Then this isn't—wasn't—purely spontaneous?'

He met her look with his own level one. 'I don't do spontaneous.'

'So the last time…?'

'Not entirely unplanned,' he granted. 'I'd been watching you shuck mussels all night, and wondered how I could get you to use those lips on me.'

She feigned outrage and went to push him off. He wouldn't budge. Her eyebrows lifted as colour piped into her cheeks.

He answered with an endearingly smug smile. 'I'm not done yet.'

She pressed her lips to his sweat-slicked shoulder, then his mouth. Their kisses forestalled conversation for some time.

Finally, his breath burned against her ear. 'So, no more Maddox?'

'I thought you were sick of talking about Brant?'

'I don't want to talk about him; I just want to hear you say it. You guys are through, right?'

Ava turned her head on the feather pillow to study him. There was no point denying it yet again. It wasn't what he wanted to know. 'We'll always be close friends.'

'Just not too close.'

'Don't you need us to…seem close? For the show?'

Dan closed his eyes, and when he opened them they were pained. 'No.'

Ava knew better. 'Yes.'

'The network needs it.'

'And you are AusOne's creature.'

He kissed her long and hard, fingers punishing her with a pinch on her still sensitised flesh. Pleasure had her muscles clamping hard around him.

Dan hissed.

'Serves you right.' Her laugh was lusty.

'I'm *your* creature,' he joked gently.

She grazed her lips across his and closed her eyes to appreciate the moment. How much would she give to have him mean that? 'I'll do whatever you need me to, Dan. I know how important this is. Maybe we could just keep it simple?'

'That didn't really work the first time. The papers have a way of turning simple into scandal.' He moved against her and they both sighed.

'Not all of them, surely? What about this one who's doing the full-length feature?'

'I've called in a few favours. Got a good journalist assigned who'll favour an angle other than what you and Maddox get up to between takes.'

Ava laughed, thinking of the games of cards, old wives' gossip and many, many cups of very unexciting coffee she and Brant had shared between shots. 'They'd be seriously disappointed with Brant and me. You and me, on the other hand...'

She pushed hard against him. His eyes fluttered shut. She kissed each lid. When they opened again they were umber. Funny how many browns there were, and how she'd learned to read them. Like a secret code.

'We can't let anyone know about this, Ava. You understand that, right?'

Ava thought about Cadence, and how many years she and Brant had kept their relationship under wraps. 'If Brant can do it, we can too.'

His head jerked back as he looked at her. 'What do you mean?'

This little titbit would have made a lot of difference to their relationship earlier. She'd withheld it intentionally. Self-defence. She took a breath. 'Brant has a long-term girlfriend who he loves desperately.'

Dan laughed. The movement caused delicious friction inside her. 'Maddox wouldn't know love if it bit him on the butt.'

'I was at the movies with her tonight. She's lovely—in a spooky kind of way.'

Dan stopped moving. Confusion and realisation filled his face. 'You're serious! But the network...the papers?'

Ava nibbled her way across his chest. 'Looks like they don't approve of Cadence. She's not TV royalty material.'

She looked at his frown and wiggled into the thick quilt. Had he truly believed that Brant was a serial sleaze? Was he as much of a victim of the network's game-playing as she was?

'The women?' he asked, bemused.

'Set up by Kurtz. Brant loves Cadence.'

Dan's mind got busy dissecting that new information. Ava snuggled closer, happy to see that he wasn't afraid of re-evaluating. 'And here's something else to blow your mind. He's smart too.'

His snort told her she'd pushed the limits of Dan's belief too far on that one. 'But he's not interested in you?'

'Only as a friend.'

'Then how smart can he be?'

He rolled suddenly, taking Ava with him so she ended up lying on top of him, her hair swinging in thick waves around her shoulders. His gaze swept appreciatively over every part of her exposed to him from this angle. She fell forward and found his mouth with hers.

'Dan?'

'Mmm?' He managed between kisses.

'Can we not talk about Brant while we…? It's kind of creepy.'

He smiled against her lips.

'My pleasure.'

CHAPTER ELEVEN

'DIONE LEEDS, *The Standard*.'

The tiny woman with cropped bleached blonde curls made a beeline straight for Ava. She dusted the dark soil off her hands and shook the offered hand. Designer outfit, overly thin, overly tanned, overly gymed, Leeds was one hundred percent yuppy. The woman couldn't have looked any more out of place amongst the earth, shrubs and flowers on the set of *Urban Nature*. Dan had chosen her because she was a journalist he trusted, but Ava didn't get a trusting vibe from this tight-faced woman.

Far from it.

'Thank you for the opportunity, Ms Lange.'

Ava smiled out of pure manners and saw the cavalry approaching. 'Don't thank me. Here comes the man who arranged it all.'

The woman stiffened, and then turned briskly and introduced herself to Dan before he could get a word out. 'You're not Lindsay Tannon,' he said.

'I'm not, no. Lindsay is ill. I'm subbing for her.'

If it was a lie, it tumbled effortlessly off Leeds' tongue. Ava would have bought it, but Dan didn't. 'The exclusive was offered to Ms Tannon. Perhaps we should reschedule—'

'No need. I'm more than qualified to stand in her place, and my substitution has been okayed by AusOne.' She met his gaze directly. 'Unless there's a specific reason you wanted Lindsay?'

Dan's lips pressed together and Ava knew they were in trouble. There were no legitimate grounds to forbid a journalist from covering the story in her colleague's place. His hands were tied. Ava was sure she could hear the sound of Dan's teeth gnashing. But outwardly he was smooth as a good red wine. If she didn't know him so well...

'Have you been briefed?' he asked.

Leeds smiled, bright and completely empty. 'Fully, thank you. Congratulations on the ATA nomination. That must be very exciting?'

'Save it for the interview.'

Ava gasped at Dan's rudeness. Surely even he would have better sense than to wave a red rag at a bull? Judging by the flash of annoyance on Dione Leeds' face, she wasn't used to being challenged.

'You have one full morning on set to observe and record, then private interviews with Ava, Maddox and myself. That should give you everything you need.'

'I may need to ask other—'

'Out of the question. Your access is exclusive, not unlimited. Ava, Maddox and myself. And we have expectations that this piece will rise a little higher than some of the exposure we've had so far.'

Leeds' face tightened in genuine offence. 'We're the *Standard*, Mr Arnot.' As though that said it all. 'I'm sure your ratings have benefited directly from that exposure, so it's a bit late now to cry poor.'

Ava swallowed nervously. Dione Leeds was every bit a match for Dan. Aggressive, on the ball, and she knew her stuff. *Damn.*

Dan signalled to one of the production assistants and the man wandered over. 'Finn, this is Ms Leeds. She'll be on-set today, researching a feature article on the show. I'd like you to stay with her, provide any assistance required, and make sure she's comfortable.'

Don't let her out of your sight. The message was clear. To all of them. He threw Leeds a tight smile.

'Ava. Can I have a word about today's schedule, please?'

They excused themselves, and Leeds got straight to work observing the set-up for the day. Her human watchdog stuck to her side.

'This is not what I had in mind.' Ava could see Dan was more agitated than he'd let on. He pushed a hand through his hair. 'I know Leeds' work. She's in a different league to Tannon.'

'That's good, isn't it? For the quality of the finished article?'

'She's an investigative reporter. A real Rottweiler. If they've sent her they must be after something bigger than we pitched.' He tore his anxious eyes off Leeds' retreating form and looked at Ava. 'I'm sorry. The interview might be harder than we expected. I'll need to warn Maddox, too. Lord only knows what he'll say.'

'Brant might surprise you. But, yes, he should be told.' She feigned a calm she really didn't feel. But Dan was agitated enough for all of them.

He swore. 'She'll almost certainly try and dig for information on you and Maddox, and it's too late to back away from the exposure we've already had. You'll have to tread a careful line with her.'

'In what way?'

'Tell her enough that she thinks she's getting somewhere, but not so much that she'll start sniffing a scoop.'

Ava had no real media training, so the idea of trying to best a professional like Leeds didn't appeal. It must have shown on her face.

His eyes softened. 'Just be yourself. Don't answer any direct questions about Maddox, but try not to evade them too obviously either.'

Oh, God. Nausea washed over her.

'You'll be fine, Ava.' His gaze caressed her. 'You can talk me in circles with your logic, so just use that.'

She wanted to touch him. To feel the reassuring pressure of his hand on hers. But her first safe opportunity was hours away yet, safely behind closed doors. After her interview slot with the Rottweiler.

Brant's secret loomed large in her mind. If even Dan hadn't known about Cadence then it was unlikely that Leeds would sniff it out, particularly if the network had gone to so much trouble to cover her up. But Ava felt the pressure of being keeper-of-the-secret. She'd need to play on the supposed romance between herself and Brant a little. But not too much. *How much was that?*

The nausea increased. How on earth had she found herself hosting a television show, being pursued by an investigative reporter and protecting someone's deeply held secrets. Three months ago she'd just been Ava Lange, country girl and landscape designer.

How much time changed things.

Brant emerged from his interview in Ava's mobile office looking slightly green around the gills and more than a little harassed. He headed straight for Ava and the coffee and doughnut she held ready for him. His hands trembled slightly when he took them from her. That worried her more than anything, because *nothing* fazed Brant Maddox. He practically downed his coffee in one.

'Cadence…?' she asked.

'No. But she's very thorough. Quite relentless, in fact.'

'What did she ask you?'

'Heaps about the programme, my vision for it. My interest in plants, for crying out loud!' Another deep sip. It must have burned, but he showed no sign. 'She wanted to know about Dan, and a heap of questions about you. Nothing particularly controversial, but still…'

As the supposed love interest for Brant, she would be a hot topic. She suggested as much to Brant. He shook his head.

'More than that. It's as if she was talking *around* the subject of me and my love-life. We talked about everything but that. And she never asked outright about you. She's too good.'

Ava's nausea increased.

'It was like the eye of the storm—like the real meaning was in the centre there, hiding inside everything else we talked about. But if you read a transcript there'd be nothing wrong with the questions.'

He took a deep breath and released it with a slow hiss. Then he blinked and refocused on Ava. 'I'm sorry, I'm scaring you to death. It wasn't all that bad, just...watch yourself. Go in knowing that she's got some kind of agenda.'

Great! 'I'm terrified she'll spring a surprise on me. That she'll know about Cadence and I'll panic and blow it for you.'

Brant balanced the doughnut on top of his coffee and put his free hand on hers. 'Hey, if that happens it won't be because you stuffed up but because she's a good journalist. Cadey and I know that we can't get away with this for ever. Don't compromise yourself to keep my secret.'

'What secret?' The Rottweiler had appeared silently behind them, a glint in her beady eyes. *Where the heck was Finn, her watchdog?*

Brant went seamlessly into charming mode. 'Shameless doughnut addiction,' he said, and took a healthy bite. He held the remnants out to admire it. 'I love these things.'

The crumbs exploding from his mouth as he spoke did the job of distracting Leeds. She looked away, disgusted. 'Ava. Are you ready?'

No. Not nearly. God, she wanted Dan by her side for this. She took a breath and smiled. 'Sure.'

A few minutes later they were in the comfort of Ava's office trailer. They'd talked niceties about the weather, the building they were renovating, the credentials of the crew. To her credit, Leeds had taken detailed notes of all the relevant discussion and politely listened to the rest. Then she got down to it.

'So, quite an amazing journey you've been on these past months. From behind-the-scenes designer to out-the-front presenter.'

Leeds' smile actually seemed genuine this time, and Ava relaxed a little. 'I still design the spaces. I consider myself a designer first.'

'The network would have to disagree with you, wouldn't they? They've invested quite a bit in you as screen talent.'

'In terms of time, I suppose. The risk of going with someone new…'

'I meant the pay-rise. The RV.' She looked around the comfortable trailer.

Ava faltered for a moment, but then remembered Dan's advice. 'This is my office. It's so I can work between takes on designs. And the pay-rise is because I'm effectively doing two jobs at once. It's not unreasonable.' Ava realised she was defending herself. Not a good start.

Leeds recovered smoothly. 'No, no—of course not. It's quite flattering when you think about it, that they felt strongly enough about you as a presenter to go to all that trouble.'

Had she ever felt flattered? Nope, not once. 'I suppose so.'

'I have to say you don't really strike me as the usual television starlet type.'

Ava forced a smile to her lips. 'I'm not. I'm a landscape designer who happens to be on television.'

'You come from…' Leeds consulted her notes '…Flynn's Beach, yes? Must be hard, being the new kid on the block in the big city, mixing in the television industry, nominated for an ATA only three months out. Pretty heady stuff—'

'The *show* is nominated.'

'And Brant Maddox.'

'He is?' That was news to Ava. Her smile was immediate and sincere. 'Oh, that's fantastic!'

Leeds looked curious. 'It was announced this morning. I'd have thought, of all people, he would have told you.'

Ava's guard shot up. 'The Brant Maddox you see and the Brant Maddox I see are quite different people. My Brant is modest enough not to brag about something like that.'

She grimaced at her own choice of phrase, and Leeds didn't miss it. Her smile was twitchingly alert. 'Your Brant?'

Despite Dan's advice, Ava couldn't bring herself to stumble through a half answer. 'If you want to ask me, go right ahead.'

Leeds didn't hesitate. 'Are you involved with Brant Maddox?'

'I'm close friends with Brant Maddox. Anything else is nobody's business but mine.' *And Dan's*.

'And Brant's?'

Ava dipped her head and conceded that point.

'Still, I would have thought that he would share this exciting news with a *close friend*?'

Ava chewed the inside of her cheek. What was the right approach here? Saying yes would be a lie, and saying no would undermine the image they'd been portraying and risk exposing Cadence.

'Perhaps he's being sensitive. Since I wasn't nominated.'

Leeds laughed. It was the most genuine thing she'd done all day. 'Sensitive? Right.'

Ava's blood boiled. Poor old Brant was going to be crucified again if she didn't speak up. She widened her eyes, all innocence. 'Oh, I didn't realise you knew Brant. He didn't mention it.'

The smile faded from Leeds' face, leaving a cold blank canvas in its place. 'I don't.'

'Well, you'll have to take it as given from someone who *does* know him that he would definitely put my feelings ahead of his own.' She managed a fair impersonation of Dan, staring Leeds down.

The woman dropped her eyes. 'Ain't love blind?' she muttered, saccharine-sweet.

Ava didn't bite. She had Leeds' number now.

Leeds shifted tack. 'Let's talk about Arnot.'

Or not. The change of subject surprised Ava. She stiffened immediately.

Leeds barrelled on. 'You seem really relaxed in his company. He must be a decent boss?'

'Because I'm relaxed around him?' Ava asked.

'And because he personally signed off on this RV.'

'Are we back to that?'

Leeds' stare was steady. 'You tell me.'

'Dan's a producer. By signing me to this deal, he got a presenter and a designer in one. I imagine it actually cost the network less, even with the pay-rise. I'd call that doing his job.'

'You defend him quite loyally.' Beady eyes grew keen.

Ava bristled. 'Why not? He deserves a little loyalty. He's been good to me.'

'Good? Feeding you on a plate to the tabloids?'

Ava's confidence stumbled, but she kept her eyes carefully screened. 'It's a producer's job to arrange publicity.'

'No, it's not, honey.' Condescension fairly dripped from Leeds' too-red lips. 'That's the publicist's job. Why is a high-level producer getting so personally involved in *your* publicity, do you suppose?'

Ava knew when she was being provoked. What was Leeds trying to imply? Her frown was genuine. 'Perhaps he's very hands-on?' she suggested.

Leeds smiled and scribbled in her notepad. 'Perhaps. You don't seem too upset about it?'

'I'm a paid employee of AusOne. If they want me to undertake PR, I'll do it. You can't imagine I'd be here with you if I wasn't required to be.'

Leeds' eager expression turned frosty. Then she struck. 'Are you involved with Daniel Arnot?'

Ava's heart stopped. She struggled valiantly to keep her expression even. When her heart started up again, it thumped so painfully in her chest she thought the journalist would surely hear it. 'Exactly how many of the men in this show am I supposed to be involved with? Perhaps you could give me a checklist to save some time? I'll just tick all those I've slept with.'

'You live in his house.'

Ava's stomach dropped. She should have predicted that one. *Stupid, stupid.* Her pulse hammered. 'I *use* his guesthouse. His completely separate guesthouse.'

'Convenient!'

'Not particularly—especially if I want to get away from work for a while.'

Leeds studied her intently. Ava met her stare as nonchalantly as she could. 'Still, not the kind of offer high-powered TV execs usually make to their employees.' Innuendo saturated the question.

Feed her a bit, but not too much. Ava had no choice. It was this or admit there was something between her and Dan. She hoped Steve would forgive her. 'It is when he's friends with the employee's brother. Her enormously over-protective brother, who wanted someone to keep an eye out for her in the big city.'

The wind billowed from Leeds' sails most effectively. She'd been completely unprepared for that answer. Her research hadn't extended to family members and their backgrounds, obviously. Ava had to fight to restrain a triumphant grin.

'Oh, I see. Okay.' Leeds cleared her throat and glanced at her notes. Silence ticked by in excruciating seconds. Then she looked up again. 'Back to Maddox.'

Too good to be true. Ava sighed. But at least they weren't talking about Dan any more.

'It occurs to me that—' Leeds picked her words carefully '—should someone want to disguise a relationship with someone...let's say someone *controversial*, then a high-profile work romance would be a great way to do it.'

Cadence. Ava's heart started thumping again. She was growing to hate Dione Leeds so much it wasn't hard to affect coolness in her answer. 'Is there a question in there somewhere?'

Leeds studied her closely, patently deciding whether to risk her next question or not. This seemed to be dangerously close to the defamation line. Ava held her breath.

'No. I guess not. Let's move on to the designs.'

Ava let air out slowly and silently, consciously trying to slow her rampant heartbeat. That had been too close for comfort. She settled in her seat and reminded herself she was in her office. Her domain.

She lowered her shoulders, quelled her churning stomach, and looked coolly at Leeds.

Bring it on.

'I guess we shouldn't be surprised she knew about you being in the guesthouse. Even Tannon would have done some homework.'

Ava was spread half across Dan as he lay on the fluffy covers of her bed—his bed, technically. She sighed. 'I hated lying.'

'What lies did you tell? Sounds to me like all you did was hedge.'

'Lying by omission.'

'That's not lying. That's politics.'

Ava muttered, realigning herself to lie next to Dan. He sounded so sure of himself. She mentally shook her head. She'd never get used to the kind of world he moved in.

She kissed the soft pads of his fingers. 'What did she ask you?'

'I think my cryptic answers frustrated her. She asked about my career, my professional pedigree—yadda-yadda. All public record stuff, so I think she was warming me up.'

'Then what?'

'Super-fast rise, string of successes. Most people compromise their integrity along the way.'

Ava knew how she would have reacted to such an insult. Integrity was as important to Dan as it was to her. 'Like *she* can talk! What did you say to that?'

'I told her that the secret was in remaining honest to your roots. That keeping close to my childhood friends was the key.'

Her lips stilled on his hands and she looked at him. 'Friends, plural?'

'No, singular. Thanks for the heads-up about Steve. Mentioning him directly took the bite right out of Leeds' attack.'

She tucked his hand into her chest. His fingers lazily traced the under curve of one breast. Tiny shivers raced across her skin. 'I didn't know what else to say,' she murmured.

'It was the right thing to say.' He gazed at the light streaming in the window and idly stroked her naked shoulder. 'I'm sorry that you have to be cagey at all—it's not how I'd like it to be. In a perfect world we could be out and proud right now.'

'Right now?' She smiled seductively.

He twisted free of her hold. 'Keep giving me that smutty little smile and I *will* be out and proud.'

His mouth found hers, putting conversation on hold while they feasted hungrily on each other. Finally he pulled free, sprinkling little kisses across her jaw before lifting his head. 'I have something to ask you.'

Dan's uncertainty intrigued her. She'd never seen him lost for words.

'Tomorrow night.' *The ATA Awards* dinner. 'I'd like… Would you…? I realise you're going anyway, but would you go with me?'

It was hard to keep the confusion from her voice. 'But don't we have to—?'

'Maddox, yes. But you and I will know…secretly…that you're with me.' Dark eyes held grey ones.

You're with me. The three most seductive words in the universe. Ava felt their impact deep in her gut, in a primal place. They entirely eclipsed those other words from her past. *I will never be with you.* She breathed deeply before answering, reminding herself that in a few months her contract would be over and she'd be returning to Flynn's Beach. She wouldn't get this chance again.

'Yes, Dan. I'd love to go with you.'

His features softened and his eyes darkened and intensified. Tension she hadn't even noticed he held drained out of him. He trailed the back of one hand over the curve of her neck. He leaned in close to her mouth and his words were almost lost in his kiss. 'Thank you.'

Every kiss just got better and better. How did he *do* that?

She sighed into his mouth and tried not to let her love show. Surely this would be enough? He didn't have to give her for ever. He laid his hand gently at her nape and shifted over her.

This would be enough.

'It's not enough!' Carrie examined Ava's flushed face critically. 'This is the Australian Television Awards, Ava. Red carpet, cameras, claws at the ready. If ever there was an occasion to break the make-up rule, it's tonight.'

'I think it's perfectly fine—'

'Perfectly bland is what it is.' Carrie bustled Ava into the bathroom, where a large mirror was rimmed with bright lights. She yanked open the marble vanity and groaned at the paucity of its contents.

'Honestly, Ava. A dress like that needs complementing, not contrasting. You're going to have to trust me on this one, okay? Do you even have mascara on?'

Ava sighed heavily, knowing it was a lost cause. The network limo wasn't due for twenty minutes; she had time to indulge Carrie. A little. 'Okay, but don't go crazy.'

There was nothing crazy about the end result. It was more make-up than she had ever worn before, but the deep slashes of copper across her eyes, the way the kohl fringed her lashes, the artful application of colour to her cheeks and jaw complemented her loaned dress perfectly.

The network had sent a rep from a fashion designer round the day before to measure up. She hadn't recognised his name, and had been duly resigned to wearing whatever minuscule monstrosity they demanded of her. But the designer had been astute, and the dress he'd sent was stunning. Exactly what she might have chosen for herself—if she'd had a choice. Modest, simple, earthy.

That last point, particularly, brought a lump to her throat. Maybe the network was finally getting her.

Moss-green fabric melted across her body, with the subtlest traces of a leaf motif, depending which way she turned in the light. A tiny clutch of embroidered leaves across one shoulder held the dress up. A mastery of hidden internal suspension held the rest of her up.

It was the most beautiful thing she had ever worn. And Carrie's magic fingers had given her a face to match. Except now... She gnawed her lip and said, 'Hair?'

Carrie glanced at her watch anxiously. 'We have time.'

They didn't, but they worked quickly together to trap Ava's locks in a creation worthy of any wedding. Forty hasty hairpins and a spritz of hairspray later, and her honey-blonde tresses finally did justice to the rest of her.

Carrie nodded with satisfaction. 'I'm going to have to sit with someone else now. So as not to be the dull one.'

Ava laughed. Carrie's plunging fire-engine-red dress was anything but dull. 'You have to sit with someone else anyway, don't you?' she teased. 'Somewhere in the cheap seats...?'

Carrie feigned outrage, her fingers reaching for the pins. 'That's it...'

Both women emerged, laughing, into the living room. Ava had left the front door open, awaiting Brant's arrival, and they saw him perfectly framed in the doorway, pulling up and clambering out of his car.

Cadence was driving.

Ava held her breath and glanced at Carrie, who looked curious but not fascinated as Brant stretched over and kissed the shadowy figure goodbye. She probably figured it was just Brant's latest pair of legs. He loped towards them across the lawn. Her heart went out to Cadence, who shouldn't have to sit out such an important occasion in Brant's career. Ava knew she must see her, standing illuminated at the front of the guest-house, and waved subtly, trying not to draw Carrie's eye.

She knew the little toot Cadence gave as she took off was as much for her as Brant.

The man in question checked out both women thoroughly. 'You both look amazing,' he said, swooping in to kiss Ava's cheek and then Carrie's.

'Don't mess the make-up!' the women shrieked together, then burst out laughing.

'Been on the champagne already?' a familiar deep voice asked.

Ava's heart flip-flopped. She turned as Dan emerged through the side gate from his property and strode towards them be-tween the gardenias she'd been training up since she'd moved in. Her throat constricted. She'd seen him in business suits plenty of times, but in a formal tuxedo—and not a cheap one—he was completely...

'Breathtaking.' Dan spoke for her, as his glowing eyes drifted over her from her gravity-defying hair to her perfectly painted toenails. She knew what a picture she must present, golden tresses piled high, neck and throat bare, figure-hugging dress and the highest of strappy high heels. There was no dis-guising the longing in his gaze. Not that he looked to be trying particularly hard.

'Hi, Dan.' Carrie's welcome was pointed.

Ava had to force her eyes away from Dan's, and she blinked to clear them. But not quickly enough. Carrie's eyes rounded in astonishment as the penny finally dropped. Her mouth fell open.

Brant, always attuned to the vibe of a crowd, broke the awk-ward silence, flattering both women and moving things along nicely with his usual panache. He looked fantastic himself in his designer tuxedo. His moss-coloured tie was a perfect match to her dress—no accident, she was sure. The network was still at it. They'd been dressed to impress, or at least to leave an impression.

Of togetherness.

You and I will know... Ava remembered a week of lazy afternoons—and late nights—and thrilled to hold that secret between them. In a room full of celebrities they would have eyes only for each other.

'Practised your acceptance speech, Maddox?' Dan said, relaxed.

'Practised yours, Arnot?'

Some of the frost had chipped off Dan's attitude since Ava had told him about Brant and Cadence. The four of them had even been to dinner together. Being public, Cadence had necessarily 'partnered' Dan. His expression on seeing her in full Goth regalia had said it all, but within the hour Cadence's amazing mind had won him over completely. He'd relaxed into an easy repartee with her and—astonishingly—she'd even blushed clear through her pale make-up at something he'd said.

Not one to hold a grudge, Brant had accepted Dan's im-proved attitude towards him gracefully. But still...boys would be boys.

Dan practically growled Brant away from Ava.

An enormous gleaming vehicle materialised out on the street, surprising them all. How something that large moved that quietly Ava didn't know. Brant was the first to the door, followed closely by Carrie, who appeared completely blasé about their transport. So did Dan.

Ava sighed. Was she the only one never to have ridden in a limo?

'You guys go on ahead,' Dan said quietly. 'I need a quick word with Ava.' He nudged the door partway closed behind Carrie.

Ava turned to him, a question on her lips, but Dan silenced it by pressing his mouth to hers. He didn't mash—sensitive, maybe, to how long it had taken to put on her awards face—but he held her tightly to him as he kissed her breath away.

Finally he raised his head. 'We can't go.'

'Why not?' Oxygen depletion robbed her of sense.

'Because I need, very badly, to kiss you again. Right now.'

His lips hovered just above hers. 'You look sensational. Did I tell you that?'

Ava smiled, not so secretly pleased. 'In a manner of speaking.'

'I picked that dress personally. I love it on you.'

She should have known. It was truly perfect.

'But I'd love it even more off you.' He kissed her again, walking her backwards towards the bedroom door. 'Except the killer heels. You can keep those on.'

She laughed against his lips, twisting reluctantly out of his grip. 'The car's waiting.'

He scooped her towards him, his hips pressed firmly against her. 'Let them wait.'

She knew he wasn't serious. He couldn't be, with two of his staff and the company limo waiting only metres away. Could he?

'Later.' Her huskiness surprised even her.

'Promise?'

She turned and teased her lips across his. 'I promise.'

A quick mirror-check later they were out through the front door, hurrying towards the idling limo.

The excitement, the glamour, the dress, Dan's closeness.

As long as she lived, she'd remember this fairytale night.

CHAPTER TWELVE

Ava didn't recognise the stocky man waiting inside the limo, but she recognised the expressions on the faces of her friends. Carrie's was pale and horrified. Brant's was furious as he stared at the newspaper in his hand.

'Bill?' Dan's voice was instantly suspicious as he pulled the door closed behind them. This man was not expected.

'The evening edition just hit the stands,' the older man said, a fevered excitement barely disguised in his eyes.

Dan reached over and took a newspaper from the seat opposite and started to read it.

The man turned to Ava. 'Bill Kurtz, Ms Lange. It's nice to finally meet you.'

Kurtz. The man who'd been making Dan's life a misery. The man who'd deemed Cadence below par. The man who'd been setting her up with the media. She took his hand reluctantly, distracted by the fury banking in Dan's eyes as he scanned the newspaper. She looked across at Brant, who was also still reading.

'That bitch…' Brant said.

Carrie reached out and put her hand on Ava's leg, sympathy etched into the sudden creases on her face. Ava's stomach plummeted.

The feature article.

'What the hell happened?' Dan exploded in the confines of the vehicle, his intensity completely focussed on Bill Kurtz.

'You tell me,' the older man said, a nerve pounding high in his jaw.

Brant threw his copy of the paper onto the empty seat in disgust, and Ava read the headline upside down.

'Unlikely starlet's success proves it's not what you know...'

She sucked in a breath. Oh, no...

'This is more than assassination, Bill. This is libel.' Dan scanned the remainder of the long article quickly.

'I imagine *The Standard*'s researchers have been all over it,' Kurtz said.

She reached for the paper and Brant stilled her hand. 'You shouldn't read it, Ava... Not tonight,' he said.

Carrie jumped in. 'She has to, Brant. She's about to walk into the lions' den.'

Ava's confused glance swung around to Dan. He raked an agitated hand through his hair and shook his head.

'I'll read it—' Kurtz offered eagerly. Dan virtually snarled at him.

'I'll read it!' Brant said, and threw Ava an apologetic glance. He lifted the paper and cleared his throat. Twice. '"Just when the status of women in media appeared to be reaching new heights, along comes a nobody from the sticks—"'

'Cow,' Carrie interrupted.

Ava blinked. Offensive, but not the end of the world. She noted Dan's pale face and Kurtz's smug satisfaction. What was she missing?

Brant read on. '"Ava Lange appeared out of nowhere onto our screens and seemed, at first take, to be a strike for real women on television. Heavier than most of her peers—",' Ava repressed her instinctive wince at that and Brant flushed red '"—but smarter and every bit as talented, she looked like a new breed in female presenters."'

Ava could feel it coming. *But...*

'"But one day in the company of Ms Lange and her sycophantic collective of supporters and it becomes clear what's really going on behind the cameras on the set of *Urban Nature*.'"

Ava met Dan's eyes and held them. Agony filled his.

"'The show reeks of nepotism, dirty secrets and spin-doctoring.'" Brant skipped ahead, touching only on the worst parts. The parts she had to hear. "'Lange is an old friend of hot-shot young producer Daniel Arnot, proving that jobs for the boys aren't restricted to those with testosterone. Arnot himself admitted to practically writing the show for Lange…'"

Ava's hands began to shake, and nausea washed through her. But her eyes never left Dan's. In her periphery, Kurtz's glare was trained in the same direction.

"'It took *The Standard*'s researchers only minutes to discover the extent of Lange and Arnot's past, and just one visit to the south coast to lock it down.'"

Ava's heart froze. They had gone to her home.

Brant paused, and skipped over a paragraph or two before resuming. "'While Arnot's past smacks of unconfirmable child abuse, Lange's was comparatively idyllic. Yet more than one Flynn's Beach local raised a question mark over the appropriateness of a teenaged Lange spending all her time with a much older Arnot. Whatever their relationship in the past, it's definitely not history…'" Brant's voice cracked as he read "'…with confirmation this week that Lange and Arnot are considerably more than friends.'"

Ava closed her eyes, frozen in her spot. She could only imagine what that confirmation was.

Dan swore. Kurtz looked at him hard.

"'Which must be a surprise to the romantically challenged Brant Maddox, who has been seen all over town with his buxom co-host… One wonders whether the gormless Maddox is aware he's being used as a cover by his apple-pie co-host, to hide a more unwholesome relationship.'"

'Enough,' Dan rumbled in the confines of the limousine.

Not Cadence and Brant. *She and Dan.* That was what Leeds

had been digging for with her questions about smokescreens and inappropriate relationships. Ava's hands trembled under Carrie's where she held them tightly. A thousand thoughts rolled through her mind, but only one was clear enough to be vocalised.

She begged Dan with her eyes. *Why?*

He swore. 'You were an easy target, Ava. I should have known better. I should have thrown her off set the moment she arrived.'

Kurtz spoke. 'That would have only stirred more suspicion and damaged AusOne's relationship with the *Standard.*'

'Screw AusOne's relationship, Bill. What about the damage to Ava?'

'That's something you should have thought about before hiring your old childhood sweetheart and moving her in under your roof!' Kurtz face glowed red with smugness. 'This disaster is all on you, Arnot.'

Dan bit back, but Ava barely heard their argument. She thought about all the work she'd done over the past few years to establish herself as a leading name in her field, to carefully build a base of credibility and goodwill. It had all disintegrated into dust. Her body started to go numb from the inside out. It helped—marginally—to keep the tears at bay.

What helped more was that in less than ten minutes she'd be getting out of the limo in front of dozens of cameras and the who's-who of the entertainment industry. The thought of doing that with a face full of shamed tears was...unthinkable.

'Stop the car. We can't go.' Carrie was definite, her focus on Ava.

Kurtz pulled rank. 'We're going.'

'If we don't go it proves Leeds right.' Brant still sounded furious.

Ava groaned and put her face in her hands. 'She *is* right.'

'She's not right, Ava,' Dan said. 'Don't give that bottom-dwelling hack the satisfaction.'

'What part of what she's written wouldn't stand up to scrutiny?' Ava pleaded with him. 'We *do* go way back. You *did* create the show around my designs. You *did* promote me to pre-senter unexpectedly. We *are* sleeping together.' Her voice rose almost to hysteria on that one. She looked at Brant. 'We *were* an item as far as the rest of the world was concerned. Regardless of the real facts, how exactly do you imagine we'll find the high ground here?'

The car dropped to frosty silence for the next kilometre. Everyone was thinking furiously as the Milana Hotel appeared in the distance. Ava's throat ached from holding the tears at bay, and from the advancing pain that had crystallised around her heart. Dan buzzed through to the driver and spoke quietly into the speaker. Almost immediately the limo slowed.

More time. As if that was going to change anything.

'What else does it say?' Her voice sounded as hollow and dead as she felt. She didn't look up, but Dan knew the question was for him.

'More of the same. She has a few things to say about my ethics. Brant gets it a few times.'

It stunned Ava out of her fog the tiniest bit to hear Dan call Brant by his given name. She met his blue eyes with a silent question.

Cadence?

Brant shook his head almost imperceptibly, but enough to let Ava know she'd managed to keep their secret. That tiny glowing light was something, at least.

'Okay,' Dan said, swinging into damage control mode. 'We can play this two ways. Close ranks. Present a united front and ride out the speculation.' He looked at Brant. 'They'll be ex-pecting you and me to be at each other's throats, so we make sure we're the best of mates tonight.'

Brant nodded and Dan continued. He leaned over and took Ava's icy hand. 'Ava, you flash that smile and keep letting it shine. You stay close to one of us at all times. Don't let anyone get you alone. Even in the Ladies' Room, you take Carrie. Someone's bound to be sniffing around for a response. We give them nothing—understood?'

'No comment,' Ava murmured. Did that actually work in the real world?

'What's the other option?' Brant asked.

'We don't go,' Dan said.

'Not an option!' Kurtz nearly choked on his own outrage.

Dan shot him a venomous look. 'If Ava wants out, I'll be with her.'

'Me too.' Brant and Carrie said together.

Kurtz turned purple, and eventually dragged his eyes to Ava. Disempowerment was clearly not somewhere he spent his summer holidays!

She considered the options. Turning around and going home was the most attractive one, but it would only delay the inevitable. She closed her eyes and took a deep breath. Walking into that crowded function room was going to be the hardest thing she'd ever had to do.

When her eyes opened the first thing she saw was Dan, the steadiness of his expression. A quiet confidence had replaced seething fury. Brant, too, looked different, his features hardening into a face that said *don't mess with me*. For the first time she recognised why Cadence leaned on him.

The limo crept along. The hotel drew closer. Ava sat taller on the plush leather seat. 'If we're going to do this, then let's do it.'

Kurtz sagged with relief and looked every bit the old man that he was.

She glared at him hard and gave him an order. 'Tell the driver to put his foot down. I want this over.'

Ava's hands still shook, and she had nowhere to hide them. As they stepped out of the limousine Dan and Brant took one hand each, as though by arrangement. It was a dangerously provocative thing to do, under the circumstances, virtually confirming the article's claims.

Yet at the same time it screamed *we have nothing to hide*, and was a clear signal to everyone watching to back off. It was a gift to have two men so experienced with the media flanking her. Gratitude for their unspoken solidarity stole a bit more of what strength she'd been able to muster.

She squeezed Dan's hand tight, drawing courage from his solid determination.

'Smile, Ava,' he whispered as they reached the edge of the dense media throng. She tried. As soon as they were spotted the cameras went crazy. The sudden barrage of flashes made the entrance of the Milana Hotel glitter like a giant diamond. Ava worked harder than she ever had to keep a brilliant smile on her face, even managing to copy a gesture or two from Brant's public repertoire.

It helped. A lot.

'You're doing great,' Dan muttered through his own tight smile. She was close enough to see fury still darkening his eyes. She knew how she looked, escorted by two burly men, and suddenly felt very much like Dorothy approaching the gates of Oz, flanked by the Tin Man and the Scarecrow. Or maybe she was the Cowardly Lion. She sure felt like it right now. She giggled weakly, entirely overwrought.

Brant threw Dan a concerned look.

Ahead, the red carpet bottlenecked into a gauntlet of television and radio presenters interviewing the beautiful people as they arrived. There was no going around it and, judging by the keen interest from the few who glanced their way, their arrival was eagerly anticipated.

'Follow my lead, hon.' Brant broke away from their defensive line and walked directly over to a tanned male presenter representing one of AusOne's major competitors. Straight into the line of fire. Dan stepped her quickly past the distracted journalist, effectively screening Ava with his wide shoulders and preventing the journalists on the other side of the gauntlet from catching her eye. It worked—for a moment.

'Ms Lange?' A young woman from an independent radio station thrust her microphone out in front of Ava so that it was virtually impossible not to stop. Dan released her hand and gently brought her to a halt in front of the woman, whispering her name to Ava. Six other microphones suddenly populated the small space between them.

'Ms Lange, are you looking forward to your first ATA awards?'

Ava knew the station by its reputation: independent music, young, switched-on presenters, philosophically resistant to commercial gossip. She realised Dan had stopped her there strategically.

She played to her strength. Directness. 'Remarkably—yes, I am, Corrine.'

She hadn't broached the subject, per se, but she'd shown she wasn't shying away from it either. The young woman smiled and pressed her luck.

'Got a battle plan this evening?' she asked.

Ava laughed lightly, practically high on adrenaline. 'First order of business is to get in there,' she said, indicating the crush ahead. 'Then to avoid any and all newspaper journalists.'

Next to her, Dan stiffened perceptibly, but the radio journo and her peers within hearing range all laughed. There was no love lost between print and broadcast media in Australia. Even Ava knew that.

'Good luck, Ava.' The woman smiled and stepped back so they could move on.

And just like that she survived her first skirmish with the media. She glanced around, risking eye contact with some of the fans in the throng. There was certainly a whole heap of interest in the stars of *Urban Nature*, and some speculation, but less judgement than she'd feared.

Much less. Her lungs loosened a little and the smile felt less forced. She paused long enough for Brant to catch up, and then proceeded, flanked again by her two bodyguards, through the press pack.

'Ms Lange…' A dozen voices juggled for supremacy. 'Mr Arnot…'

Someone screamed Brant's name from the rear of the throng, and Ava's laugh was genuine. This was her first taste of hard-core fans, but Brant played them like a Stradivarius. If she were ever to survive something like this again, she'd need lessons from the Maddox School of Media Training.

She stumbled slightly on the thought. Since when was she even considering sticking around long enough to do this ever again? Was the adrenaline affecting her judgement?

'Nearly there.' Dan guided her with a steady hand, and she saw the red carpet widen out ahead, and then the gaping entry to the Milana's glamorous function room beyond it. His hand burned against her bare skin and he softly stroked his thumb across her hip. She would never have managed this without him. She owed him—owed them both. Except Brant's thank-you would be more in the order of a good bottle of wine, whereas Dan's...

She chuckled. Then laughed again when Dan's eyes narrowed. He probably thought she was losing it.

He wasn't far wrong.

They stopped twice more, bypassing certain journalists and favouring others. Brant stole the show, gracing the press with his full attention and taking the heat off Ava. He brushed aside the few tactless comments made by less courteous media, and easily shepherded the interviews into less awkward territory. Since he was the one supposedly scorned, they were more careful with him than they would have been with her.

It baffled the heck out of all of them that the three were being so supportive and friendly with each other after what they'd read in *The Standard*.

Ava didn't get off completely, though she found herself able to answer questions more easily now that she knew the throng wasn't out to lynch her, specifically. Her heart-rate slowed to a steady thump, then spiked when a gorgeous-smelling Dan bent close to her ear.

'Last stop, Ava. Get ready.'

An honest-to-goodness supermodel—now a key presenter for AusOne's rival network—stood at the top of the sweeping stairs leading to the doors of the hotel function centre. Ava realised with a rush what was coming up.

The fashion corral.

She'd watched this part of the ATA ceremony in her pyjamas a hundred times. All the beautiful people passed through the corral, showing off their designer creations and answering questions.

Live to air.

Her mouth dried and she scrabbled around in her muddled brain for the name of her designer. Reluctantly Dan released her hand and dissolved into the background, leaving her to face it alone. She felt bereft at the tiny betrayal. Then suddenly Brant swept in beside her and took her arm.

Better than nothing. His grin was wide and flashing enough for both of them as he greeted the supermodel.

'Ava, Brant. Lovely to see you both this evening.' The model plied her trademark smile generously. Ava blinked in the bright light from the camera pointing at them. She didn't want to think about it being live to air. If this woman chose to say something shocking, she'd have no hope of covering her reaction. Brant slid an arm around her and tucked her closer to his side.

'You both look fantastic. Who's your designer?' A microphone was thrust towards her. Ava opened her mouth and prayed something intelligent was going to come out. Lord, who *was* her designer?

'Glenn Lo.' Oh, thank the stars! 'I think he's picked the perfect dress for me.' She sucked in a nervous breath.

'You look magnificent,' the presenter said. 'And what a lucky girl—a gorgeous man on each arm, and a third one gifting you fashion.'

Allusions, but no direct attack. In fact there was a strange glint of solidarity in the supermodel's eye. Ava scrabbled in her memory banks. Wait—was this the woman whose ex had put a video on the internet…?

The model turned to the camera and winked. 'We should all be so lucky! Speaking of luck—all the very best, Brant, for your category tonight.'

Seconds later, miraculously, it was over. The three of them stood patiently for the compulsory publicity shots in front of the sponsor's signage, and then were shooed into the darkened auditorium.

Ava's legs began to weaken as soon as they were in the shadows. The adrenaline dissipated, leaving her wobbly. 'I think I should sit…'

'Hang on, Ava.' Dan was right there beside her, his hand sliding around her waist. He signalled to Brant, who snagged an elegant chair from nearby and placed it deep into the shadows of a recess. She sank gratefully into it and the two men closed ranks in front of her, facing the crowd, bodies relaxed, as though they were having a casual conversation.

Dressed as she was, putting her head between her knees was out of the question. She settled instead for letting it sag while she sucked in great a lungful of designer air. *I can't do this.* Impossibility washed over her. Who would notice if she tiptoed out now? As long as Brant stayed for his award, Dan, too, for *Urban Nature*'s…couldn't she go?

No, someone would make it their business to notice. And to speculate.

United front, Dan had said. And not just for her sake. They'd all been tarnished by Leeds' shameful article. She should remember that.

Child abuse. Leeds' allegation suddenly came into clear focus in her mind. Dan's father…

Her heart ached for the frightened, lonely little boy Dan must have been if it was true. There was no way she was going to repay his courage by leaving now.

She flexed and un-flexed her fingers, noticing their tingling for the first time. Had she been numb since getting out of the limo? The natural chemicals zinging around her system had made her oblivious to anything but survival. Like getting through the media pack in one piece. Now that she had, her body's defences were easing off and pain was returning. Her jaw ached from its rigid smile and her rib muscles were tender from being held so tight.

'Ava?' Dan's voice was loud enough to carry to her, but not so loud it would draw any attention. She sighed, knowing she couldn't stay here all night, expecting them to cover for her. It wasn't fair to them. They'd been amazing to get her this far.

'I'm ready.' She stood and stepped into the gap that opened between them.

The function room was exquisitely decorated, and filling rapidly with Australian and international guest celebrities as well as producers, filmmakers, crew and their partners. Ava scanned the room but saw no sign of Leeds. Maybe the press were still caught up out at the front.

She relaxed a little, shaking off her nerves and smiling shakily at Dan. 'Shall we find our table?'

The first part of the evening wasn't being televised. Ava was embarrassed to discover they'd arrived well after the earliest awards were read out. She felt affronted on behalf of those people who'd worked hard for their place on the awards list but whose achievement was barely acknowledged by the handful of assembled guests. There seemed to be a category for everything—theme music, catering, costume, make-up, even commercial risk finance.

None of them sexy enough for broadcast, apparently.

She paid particular attention to every one as penance for her late arrival, and in solidarity for the little people. As far as she was concerned she was still a behind-the-scenes person at heart. Dan smiled when he realised what she was doing and patiently sat with her, attending to the activity on stage with just as much focus as she.

How could she ever have thought him disloyal?

For another thirty minutes other distinguished guests continued to stream into the venue, upstaging the award presentations onstage. The later the arrival, the higher the standing in the industry, it seemed. Ava was too exhausted to care as some big name Hollywood types strolled past them just minutes before the start.

Carrie caught up with her briefly and pointed out where her table was. Just as Ava had joked, it was right at the back, near the restrooms. The mere thought of the word had Ava thinking about her bladder, and she excused herself quietly.

'Take Carrie,' Dan ordered.

Although one or two seemed to consider it, no one actually approached—thanks largely to Carrie's excellent impersonation of an Alsatian. Every time someone came too close, she swung her body around and glared at them.

'You'll be growling next,' Ava laughed, soaping her hands.

'This whole business has me so mad,' Carrie whispered fiercely under her breath. 'Of all the people, Ava. *You?* There couldn't be a nicer person to work with in this entire industry. You make coffee for the crew, for goodness' sake. Who else does that? I just don't understand it.'

Carrie's rigid defence thawed a bit more of Ava's frozen heart. She'd really lucked out finding this woman as a friend. She squeezed Carrie's fingers with her own lavender-scented ones.

'I'm so pleased I met you, Carrie Watson. I hope we get to work together for years.'

Years? Ava shook her head to banish the thought. *Not years…months…weeks.* She was going home in a few months.

They stopped by Carrie's table so Ava could say hello to the rest of the *Urban Nature* crew present. Most gave her a supportive smile, but one or two had clear speculation in their guarded expressions. Ava sighed sadly, then turned to Carrie. 'You might as well take your seat. I'm hardly likely to get accosted between here and our table.'

Carrie started to argue, until she saw the determined look on Ava's face. She relented, saying, 'Fingers crossed for both awards, then?'

The awards. Ava had almost forgotten the whole reason for being here tonight. Nervous butterflies launched in her belly. She wondered how Brant was feeling. And Dan. It was an important achievement for them both. She moved smoothly and quickly towards her table, avoiding eye contact with everyone just in case. The last thing they needed was some kind of public incident.

Another public incident.

Dan sat at the table next to Bill Kurtz. Brant's seat was still empty while he was off schmoozing. Ava frowned, and the hairs on her arms prickled. There was something about Dan's posture... He sat rigid in his seat, and Kurtz leaned into him like a vulture picking over a carcass. With their backs to her, neither man noticed her approach. There was a momentary lull in the music blaring over the PA system and she heard Bill Kurtz's booming voice distinctly.

'...never mind your own reputation. I don't give a toss about that. You put the network at risk, the shareholders, for a piece of skirt.'

Dan's body language turned from frigid to fiery in a blink. 'You couldn't help yourself, could you, Bill? You haven't shared a limo in ten years, but you were willing to make a concession if it meant a ringside seat to watch the fall-out of your handiwork first-hand. You're nothing but an ambulance-chaser—'

Ava couldn't see Kurtz's face, but his entire body stiffened. 'Then what are you, Arnot? A man willing to sell his woman out to the media even while you were sleeping with her? Have you told her yet that it was *you* that sold her out, or is all this holier-than-though crap just lip-service?'

Dan surged to his feet. People at neighbouring tables turned to look.

Ava stumbled to a halt. Her heart struck cold. She instantly recalled Dione Leeds' snarky comment about Dan arranging the various PR incidents. And then an image came—Dan outside in the shadows on the night the restaurant photo had been taken, the incorrect call sheets, the ones Dan had handed them personally, Dan speaking with the *maître d'* just before she and Brant were *accidentally* seated at the wrong table, a romantic table for two by a bright open window. Where a photographer had just happened to see them. The first photo that had started it all.

Worse, Dan had been at every publicity event since she'd started on-camera with *Urban Nature*.

Her skin prickled into tiny bumps. What was it she had said about the publicity? *Engineered.* Crystals of ice immediately encased her heart.

'Is that true, Dan?'

Both men snapped around, but only one looked appalled to find her standing there. Bill Kurtz just looked smug. Ava ignored him entirely; her narrowed eyes were fixed in despair on the handsome face in front of her, on the man who had always had the power to hurt her. The man who looked one hundred percent guilty as charged.

'Ava...' Dan started towards her as another song started on the massive PA system. It was a soggy love-song that any other night she would have hummed happily along with. Now she'd forever associate it with the feeling of her heart being torn from her body.

She flung two hands in front of her, stopping him. They shook with the effort of keeping her voice level. *'Is. That. True?'*

He glued a phony smile to his face and stepped towards her.

'Don't do this, Ava. People are watching,' he muttered through the grimace, grabbing her arm and steering her towards the half-empty dance floor. It was about as private as they would get with all these industry types around.

She went into his arms as comfortably as a sacrifice went unto death, and then looked at him through a wash of unshed tears. A giant fist squeezed her heart and stole her ability to speak. She didn't need to; he knew what she wanted to know.

'Hold on, Ava. There are a thousand eyes here.' He pulled her slowly around the dance floor and Ava struggled to regain some composure. Finally he spoke. 'I should have told you. I'm sorry.'

Ava didn't know whether to be grateful he was holding her up or horrified to be touching him. Every word he'd ever said to her suddenly turned to ash. She forced sound over her frozen lips.

'What have you done?'

He sighed. 'It was part of my job.'

'To sell me out to the media? Part of your job?'

She saw him wince, but her heart had no room left for pity. A deep-seated coldness spread outwards from the dying organ. 'You kept forcing me and Brant together.' It wasn't a question and it didn't need an answer. He didn't give her one. 'The restaurant. Was that you?' she grated.

He didn't nod. But he didn't deny it. His eyes were fixed over her shoulder. His grasp tight.

'All those other stories?' Unshed tears choked her throat.

He shook his head. 'No. But I started the feeding frenzy. I made that choice.'

Sharp hurt roiled deep in her belly.

'The first one was really all that was needed,' he said quietly. 'It whetted the public appetite for more. Then Kurtz took over.'

She took a deep breath and spoke through the hurt. 'You let them do this to me? To Brant?'

'No, Maddox knew.'

Wham. A double hit of agony. 'Brant knew. You knew. The network knew. Seems like the only chump not to know was little ole Ava from the sticks.'

'Ava, don't…'

She wrenched free, unable to stomach his hands on her for a second longer. 'Is he that powerful, Dan? Your father?'

He paled and looked away. 'He has nothing to do with this.'

'He has everything do to with this. You chose him over me. You made revenge on him more important than what we have.' She caught herself. Her chest heaved. '*Had*. Past tense.'

The romantic music played on. Dan struggled to keep his composure. 'You don't mean that.'

Ava straightened her spine, amazed it didn't snap under the strain. 'Completely.'

'Without even letting me explain?'

'Oh? You can explain? Go ahead.' She stared at him hard as he moved her automatically around the dance floor. His mouth opened and shut several times until finally his eyes dropped away. 'How did you expect me to react?' she whispered.

Dan sighed and tucked her in closer, as though she might break away. It was hard to know if the lights overhead were spinning or if it was just her.

'Like this,' he sighed. 'You have every right to be angry.'

'I am so much more than angry.' She curled her hands into fists. Wanting to hit him. Wanting him to hurt as much as she was hurting right now. 'I'm broken, Dan.' Her voice cracked.

Bleakness streaked through his eyes. 'Ava, please understand the position I was in. Wanting to do the best thing by everyone. I swear on your mother's grave, I was trying to protect you—'

'A wise man once told me to grow a spine. Well, how about doing the same and standing up for someone you love?' A tear escaped down her cheek just as a booming voice came across the public address system, announcing the commencement of the televised portion of the awards. Guests streamed towards their seats. 'Oh, that's right. It's only lust, isn't it? I doubt you're even capable of love. Look at the role models you had.'

She turned to go. Dan held her wrist and dragged her to him, eyes glittering. 'Nine years ago you accused me of being just like my mother. Of running out when the going got too tough. Well, what are *you* doing now, Ava?'

She stared at him in horror. Apparently even at sixteen she'd known enough to strike exactly where it would do most damage. And it had, if he'd hung onto it all this time.

'I can't understand why hurting him is so important to you,' she whispered. 'Tell me. Help me understand.'

The plea hung between them. Agony filled his eyes. Then his voice was quiet. Hard. 'I don't have room for anything else inside me, Ava. There's nothing left in there except raw hatred for that man and what he did to me. It has sustained me for years.'

She stared at him, appalled by the emptiness in his eyes. No wonder he'd had a string of meaningless relationships. No wonder he was so driven to succeed. It was all he had.

'No, Dan. It has sustained *itself* for twenty years. Like a parasite sucking all the worth out of your life. It's consumed everything you loved.' She twisted her wrist from his hand. 'First you fed it surfing. Now you're feeding it me.'

His eyes glassed over. Toughened as she watched. 'I don't have anything more to offer you, Ava.' He released her away from him. 'I'm empty. I don't know how to be any other way.'

The lights started to dim and the room hushed. She stumbled behind him to the table and grabbed her seat for support just as Brant slid in next to her. She was directly opposite Dan. No coincidence. After all, they were supposed to be giving each other secret cow-eyes across the table all night.

What a joke.

The pain of betrayal sliced through her in the gathering hush. She sensed Brant's confusion when she gave him the cold shoulder, too. The evening stretched interminably ahead of her, seated at a table full of men who had either betrayed her or were using her.

Or both.

The lights dimmed, the glitterati hushed, and a booming voice burst over the crowd. 'Ladies and gentlemen, welcome to the forty-sixth Annual Australian Television Awards gala dinner…'

Ava looked around at the excitement, the anticipation of those seated on other tables. It should have been like that for her. Seated across from the man she loved, celebrating his success, knowing she had contributed to it.

Instead, here they were. Dan's eyes cold and remote, staring away from her. The slimebag Kurtz savouring his victory. Her own heart bleeding out onto the expensive carpet.

It physically hurt to breathe. Was the tug-of-war between loving someone and hating them what made hearts break?

Brant won his category—Best Male Talent in a Non-Drama Role. She might still be mad at him, but it was impossible not to feel some happiness for him. Despite everything people said or thought about him, Brant Maddox was adored by the voting public. The applause from the public seats was thunderous testament to that.

Ava met Brant's eyes a split second before he stood from the table, suddenly unable to punish him further for something he couldn't control. It just felt wrong. She smiled encouragement at him, and the sheer relief in his expression only served to intensify her guilt. This was his night and she was blowing it for him. What Cadence wouldn't give to be here in her place...

Brant casually moved to the stage, stopping to shake a hand or two and slap a shoulder or three on the way. His acceptance speech was short and to the point. And one hundred percent loaded for those in the know.

'And to my heart,' he finished, pulling his statuette against the left side of his chest, 'only you know what this really means to me, and only you really know me. Thank you.'

He hadn't looked at anyone in particular, but half the room glanced at Ava. Onstage, Brant blew a kiss to the camera as though it was for his fans. But Ava knew better.

She blinked away tears and glanced up, only to find Dan's burning regard on her. She forced her eyes back to the stage.

Kurtz and a nameless AusOne executive were congratulating themselves on their achievement. Ava's stomach turned. As though their intensive meddling at Cadence's expense had *anything* to do with Brant's own success. He'd got his nomination *despite* their involvement, not because if it.

Brant left the stage via the wings as the show broke for its first commercial break, and then appeared across the room through a backstage door. Out of nowhere, a roving camera appeared at their table and was thrust into Ava's face. She was entirely unprepared. Dan stretched forward, too late to ward it off.

'Ava, that was quite a speech. How does it feel to be so publicly affirmed?'

Exhaustion, misery and anger all warred within her—but all she could think about was Cadence. How she must feel, sitting in her living room watching all this happen without her. Watching the man she loved face his biggest career moment alone. Watching another woman seated in her rightful place.

Ava swallowed her pain and spoke from the soul, the weight of Brant's secret an extra strain on her weary heart, hoping that Cadence was still watching. She turned towards the camera shoved in close to her face, knowing her eyes would be glittering dangerously from the unshed hurts of the evening. 'There's not a woman alive who wouldn't be moved to tears at having her love so publicly validated.' The tiniest of pauses. 'If it was directed at her.'

She threw Brant a watery smile as he arrived at the table, gold paperweight in hand. The cameraman and the presenter exchanged confused looks at her cryptic answer, then turned their attention on the man of the moment.

Ava let Brant enjoy the spotlight. He'd earned it. She glanced briefly across the table to where Dan studied the tablecloth intently. Then his eyes jerked up and locked with hers, blazing and sharp.

Rib-spreaders couldn't have done a better job of baring her pulped heart.

Dan rose suddenly from his seat and walked away, just as the lights dropped again for the next televised segment. Brant watched her watching Dan go.

'What did I miss?' he whispered over the introduction to the next segment.

She shook her head.

'Ava...?'

She spun around, hurt. 'Why didn't you tell me about the publicity? That Dan was behind it?'

'Ah.' He considered her for a moment. 'What would it have changed?'

'I would have known.'

'And that would have been better how?'

'Because then maybe I wouldn't have found out this way.' Her voice was tiny.

Brant dropped his eyes. 'True. But none of us could have predicted this.'

She looked at him. His judgement and his industry savvy were solid. 'You don't think all this was part of Dan's plan?'

He looked shocked. 'No. Do you?'

Ava hesitated at his certainty, and then shrugged.

'Hon, I saw his face in the limo,' Brant said. 'It was not the face of a man who knew what was coming. He was as pole-axed as the rest of us.' He nodded towards Kurtz, who was watching the proceedings on-stage with interest. 'That face, on the other hand...'

Ava considered. 'You think Kurtz knew which way the story was going to go?'

'Dan believed I was a womanising git, remember? And Kurtz is threatened by him.'

She couldn't join the dots. Her mind was too jumbled for any more puzzles. 'So?'

'It means the network didn't fill him in—didn't tell him all the women were a screen for Cadence. They didn't trust him, Ava. I think Kurtz did this whole thing to stick it to Dan, primarily. To establish his dominance.'

The layers of deceit were baffling. It was almost impossible to sort out who meant what. She'd even indulged in a little spin of her own, covering for Cadence. She'd been a willing participant in most of the PR, made it all too easy for Dan to arrange what the network wanted. She'd put up no resistance at all.

'Please understand the position I was in,' he'd said. *'Trying to protect you.'* Maybe he'd been working from day to day with what information he'd had at the time. Trying desperately to control the outcome. While Kurtz had worked behind the scenes screwing him over, too.

With sudden insight she began to see everything from Dan's perspective. Wangling her the pay-rise and the RV to compensate for forcing her hand; supporting her refusal to wear the skimpy outfit; constantly on set to keep control of things; trying to negotiate a decent reporter for the feature article; his absolute fury when that hadn't come off.

Trying to spin the spin. All the while trying desperately to hang on to the only thing that meant anything to him on this planet. His career.

She stared blankly at the stage as the facts slotted into place. Then she looked around for him, suddenly desperate to speak with him alone. To get more answers. To listen. To trust. She saw the big double doors open a crack and a set of broad shoulders slip out into the foyer.

Dan.

Before Brant even knew she was gone, she was threading quickly through the crowded tables towards the exit. She ignored Carrie's signal to her and pushed through into the foyer alone. She glanced around. Empty, save for a few waiting staff doing their thing, bussing dirty dishes out to the kitchen. Surely he wouldn't leave? Not before his category? Her heart lurched at the thought. She hurried to the entrance of the auditorium and peered around outside.

Then she froze as she heard the one voice she'd been avoiding all night.

'Well, well. If it isn't the country mouse.'

CHAPTER THIRTEEN

DAN slid into his chair and tossed his rolled-up napkin at Maddox, who looked around in surprise in the dark. 'Where's Ava?' he hissed over the hubbub from nearby tables.

Brant shrugged and mouthed the words *ladies' room*.

Why wasn't Maddox keeping an eye out for her? That was his job! *No, it is your job*, a tiny voice reprimanded. He'd lost his cool for a moment—had to get out before he did or said something he'd regret. The pain in her body language had nearly killed him.

He'd left Ava alone and unsupported while she was still desperately struggling.

She was beyond angry—any idiot could see that. She was confused and hurting, and all because of him. His gut had warned him to tell her about the PR stunts earlier. To explain on his own terms. There'd even been a time or two where the conversation had naturally lent itself to a full confession, but he'd chickened out. He'd been afraid she'd walk away, tell him it was over. As she just had.

And that possibility terrified him.

Not that he didn't understand. Ava had been stretched about as far as any human being could go tonight. He hoped in his heart she'd spoken only from anger and hurt, and that both might pass once he got a chance to talk to her. To explain every detail.

Every humiliating, painful detail.

She deserved at least that. And, frankly, he was tired of carrying it all by himself. He'd told her he was empty, had no room for her. But the weeping hole left now that she'd walked away from him proved that wasn't true.

Somehow, some time over the past few months, Ava Lange had worked her way into his heart and staked a claim. Displaced some of the darkness.

He wasn't going to lose the only constant love he'd had in his life.

He craned his neck to monitor both sets of doors leading from the auditorium. Where was she? Onstage, the presenter ran through the nominations for Best New Lifestyle Programme and short snippets of each were played on the giant screen behind him. Dan's heart gave a lurch to see Ava, one hundred times enlarged on the massive screen, looking so fresh and beautiful. The contrast with how he'd seen her moments ago was marked.

A gnawing feeling settled into his gut.

'And the winner of the Best New Lifestyle Programme is…'

Dan twisted his neck and stared at the exit doors. What if she hadn't gone to the ladies' room?

Where was she?

Ava pushed past Dione Leeds and headed for the restrooms, not trusting herself to speak. Leeds followed her into the ladies' lounge, where a number of comfortable seats and a viewing monitor were set up so guests could keep track of what was happening on stage as they used the facilities.

'Nothing to say now, Ms Lange? That's certainly a change from our interview.'

Ava spun around to face her nemesis. 'Is that what this is about? You didn't like the way I spoke to you?'

The journalist laughed. 'Oh, please, don't flatter yourself.'

'Then what? What exactly do you have against me, particularly? You don't even know me.'

Dan's voice came to her. *We give them nothing.* But she couldn't do it; there was too much fight in her. She was a pressure cooker ready to blow.

'I know your type.' Leeds glared at her coldly. 'I had to work damn hard to get where I am, and I had to scrabble my way over the corpses of women like you who slept their way into cushy positions and then couldn't pull their weight. It fell to the rest of us to pick up the slack. Meanwhile we got overlooked time and again for advancement because we were too busy covering someone else's ass.'

Ava heard the desperation behind Leeds' words, but she was incapable of compassion. That was a first. She gathered all the hurts, fears and disappointments since she'd climbed, innocent and excited, into AusOne's limousine and pushed them out at an unsuspecting Dione Leeds. A woman who had probably figured her for an easy target.

'And is this the kind of story you hope will bring you advancement? A sleazy story about the private lives of people who work in television? This is what passes for ace reporting at *The Standard*?'

Leeds greyed at the gills and was finally speechless. Strength surged through Ava, uncontrolled and wild, but she was determined that Leeds was about to reap exactly what she'd sown.

'You could have written a great business story about Australia's youngest executive producer in waiting. Or done a serious piece on the real issues facing communities who are living their lives in natureless urban environments. Instead you went for a cheap shot, thinking you were onto some sordid scoop. And you signed your name to it like it was something to be proud of!'

She careened on like an out-of-control train. 'After tonight everyone will remember you for a trashy piece you did on some lifestyle presenters. They'll forget all the meaningful articles you've ever written in that long, hard climb to the top. And, worse, your paper's hardly going to reward you when

AusOne sues you for defamation—because, although you got some basic facts right, you've put them together wrong. Bill Kurtz might be a powerful man, and he might have promised you the earth, but Daniel Arnot is the future of that network and he has silent support higher up the food-chain than Kurtz or he wouldn't have come this far. What you've printed is fundamentally lies, Ms Leeds. And we'll prove it.'

Ava's voice was clear and unwavering, and that, more than anything, was Leeds' undoing. The woman paled even further, and then pulled herself up to her full tiny height, turned on her heel and marched out without saying another word. She pushed past Carrie, who stood, agog, in the doorway.

'You were fantastic, Ava!' she squeaked.

Ava felt the rush of a crisis passed, and sank into one of the comfortable armchairs in the lounge, trembling. She felt as if that was all she'd done all night.

'Are you okay?' Carrie slipped a warm hand over her cold one.

'I will be,' Ava said with certainty. 'If I survive this night, I can survive anything.'

The two of them sat in companionable silence, staring unseeing at the television until Brant and then Ava's face appeared briefly on screen, along with the presenters of three other popular lifestyle programmes.

Carrie gasped. 'It's our category.' She deactivated the mute button on the remote just as the announcer spoke.

'And the winner of the Best New Lifestyle Programme is...'

'...*Urban Nature!*'

Before his boss could do more than button his blazer Dan was on his feet, striding toward the stage. He didn't need to look behind him to know Kurtz would be livid. There was an unspoken rule at AusOne. The staff did all the work. The executives took all the glory.

Dan took the steps to the stage two at a time, and moved straight into an air-kiss with the gorgeous starlet who had presented the category. He accepted the award statue, and then waited for the courteous applause to settle.

'Thank you, on behalf of AusOne and the hardworking cast and crew of *Urban Nature*.' Someone yelled *woo-hoo* way up at the back. 'It's my absolute pleasure to accept this award for the network that gave me my start in this business.'

More polite applause, then the audience fell to silence. Dan looked at the shiny gold statue in his hands, and then squinted out into the lights that obscured most of the avid faces. It wasn't hard to forget they were there, such was the hush in the room. He visualised his father sitting in the front row, a knowing smirk on his face, having waited for empirical evidence that his son really was a loser.

Not any more, Dad.

'There's a reason I chose to work in lifestyle television instead of drama. I much prefer reality to the kind of constructed fiction others thrive on.' His heart pounded so hard it hurt. 'However, recent events have made my very successful, very enjoyable, very *credible* lifestyle programme seem more like daytime television.'

Someone coughed out in the dark. No one else so much as shuffled.

'Dione Leeds would do very well over in your drama department, Marcus Croyden—' Dan turned towards the right, where he knew the head of a rival network with a stable of highly successful soap operas was seated '—such is her talent for stretching a few basic facts into a work of sensational fiction.'

A gasp from the crowd this time.

Dan's nostrils flared. 'You think that's a bit bold? I'm only getting started.'

He had time. The floor manager of this broadcast would lose his job if he cut to a commercial or played the wind-up music now. This was the stuff ratings were made of. Dan could practically feel the cameras zooming in. After all, how often did someone commit career *hara-kiri* live on stage?

'Tonight, part of my job was to help perpetuate the idea that Ava Lange and Brant Maddox are involved—caught up in a great love affair which has blossomed since the show started production. It's something the network has been eager to promote. The trouble is Brant and Ava aren't in love. At least, not with each other. Somewhere out there in the suburbs, watching this broadcast, is a sweet and unconventional woman who would lay down her life for Brant Maddox. She already has, in agreeing to virtually disappear because she doesn't fit the mould of celebrity accessory.' All his affection and admiration for Cadence was revealed in his wide grin. 'She is the love of Brant Maddox's life, and he's paid a huge personal price trying to protect her from the sharks of this industry. I hope next year you'll see her, sitting there at the AusOne table, looking surly and frightening people.'

Brant laughed loudly from his seat. There was approval, relief and gratitude in that laugh.

'Cadence.' Dan's eyes found the camera with a red light on and he looked down its barrel. 'For my part in what's been done to you I can only apologise, and hope you'll forgive me.' He turned his head in Brant's direction. 'I could learn a lesson or two from Brant Maddox about loyalty and about love.' He let that one sink in with the audience. 'And Ava Lange? Well, she's in love, too. *With me.* Or at least I hope so, because I'm absolutely crazy about her.' This earned a chuckle from the crowd. 'It's true I've known her for half my life, but here's a quote you won't have seen on today's newsstands...'

He swallowed hard.

'Ava Lange did not get involved with me to get this role. In fact, she did everything she could *not* to take on the hosting role. I manipulated her into taking the job—just like I manipulated her into participating in this façade with Brant Maddox. Both of which are things I'll have to live with. As it happens, Ava also did everything she could *not* to be with me, but fortunately I prevailed.'

Gentle laughter grew, moving like a Mexican wave through

the audience. Dan felt their loyalty shift. He scanned the sea of dimly lit faces in the room until his eyes stumbled upon a lone female figure silhouetted against the light from the foyer streaming in the open door behind her. He would have recognised that stubborn, proud, vulnerable stance anywhere. He stared hard across the hundreds of heads and swallowed nervously. In his periphery, he saw a camera swing one hundred and eighty degrees to see what had grabbed his attention.

He took a breath and took a chance.

'Ava Lange, every time you smile a monkey is born in a forest somewhere. When you're sad, oceans ice over. When you laugh, flowers burst into bloom. You are so intrinsically linked to nature it responds to your moods. And I'm so intrinsically linked to you I can't imagine a life with anyone else. Or a life without your beauty in it.'

Every female in the room sighed.

His energy reached out to find hers. 'I put some really dark emotions ahead of you, even after vowing to protect you for ever. That's on me, and I swear I will do everything I can to fix the damage I've caused. If I hadn't been so blinded by ancient anger I might have seen your radiance sooner. I'm done with proving myself to someone who means nothing to me. I'm moving on to proving myself to someone who means everything to me.'

He shifted more firmly on his feet and cleared his throat. 'You deserve your design spot on *Urban Nature* because you have a unique talent and a world of professional integrity. You deserve your spot as presenter because the public respond so magnificently to your passion for wild things. What you don't deserve is what's happened to you today. For doing nothing less than helping out a friend—' he looked at Brant '—and putting my needs ahead of your own—' then at Kurtz '—you've been judged and publicly executed.'

Dan rounded on the audience and held up the golden statue. 'So, thank you again to the people of Australia who responded to all the good things about our programme. I hope you keep watching. Not to see what the latest scandal of the day is, but to see us give derelict spaces back their soul. And to everyone here tonight I'd ask you to put yourselves in the shoes of a sweet and gentle woman from the southern coast who was crucified in the interest of ratings and newspaper sales. Because it could just as easily be you next. Thank you.'

The applause started slowly, but as Dan marched down the steps of the stage the ovation grew. A few in the audience even leapt to their feet. It seemed there were more than a few people present who were happy to see a network—and some aspects of the media—called to task for their game-playing.

Dan's eyes sought out the lonely silhouette, and he triangulated the fastest route to her through the crowd.

He paused at the AusOne table only long enough to meet Brant's approving gaze briefly and to dump the prized statuette in front of Bill Kurtz.

'I quit!' he shouted over the noise.

'No need,' Kurtz snarled. 'You're fired.'

As exits went, it wasn't particularly dramatic—he had to weave in and out of tables—but it did mean he passed a number of other network tables. At one, a slim, greying man reached out to shake Dan's hand and subtly pressed a business card into it. Dan glanced at it—X-Dream Sports, the biggest cable sports network in Australia. The largest broadcaster on the surfing circuit in the world.

'I assume you're on the market?' the man mouthed over the din as Dan passed.

He tucked the card away safely.

More and more of the audience turned to follow him with their eyes, until they were all facing the rear of the auditorium. An excited murmur rose beneath the applause as they recognised the woman standing at the exit. It felt like surfing, the way he was carried towards her on a wave of her name on strangers' lips. She stepped forward into the light. So serious and beautiful. His eyes held hers as he approached, agonisingly slowly.

Carrie tactfully disappeared from behind her with a sisterly squeeze of her arm, leaving the two of them to be the absolute centre of public attention.

He didn't care. For once in his life the only thing driving him was the woman standing before him.

Finally she was close enough to touch, and he stopped in his tracks. Most of the crowd around them hushed.

She raised a hand towards him…

…and punched him in the arm.

Hard.

'Ava!' Dan rubbed his bruised bicep, his eyes the mocha colour of surprise.

'What did you do?' She punched him again and he dodged out of the way. Her heart squeezed so hard she could only suck in tiny breaths. 'Did you just throw your career away?'

'I did what I had to, Ava. I had to choose. And I choose you.'

Tears threatened, but she fought them back. 'You threw your whole career away—everything you've worked for…'

'Which is meaningless if I have no respect for myself.'

'For me?' The words barely squeaked out. Her throat couldn't do much else, tight as it was with unshed tears. Love welled dangerously close to the surface.

'No,' he said. 'For us. I couldn't ask you to stay with all that hanging over you. I had to set the record straight.'

'It was so…' She groped for the right word. Tears brimmed.

'Stupid?' he smiled.

'Spectacular.' She stepped forward and fell into his arms, his kiss. The people at the tables nearest to them cheered. A lighting tech high in the rig spun the spotlight away from the stage and towards the doors, to bathe them in glorious luminescence. It had the added effect of making most of the audience vanish into shadow. It was a strange, ethereal kind of privacy.

Dan broke away and set Ava back a step. Her overwhelmed

chest heaved as she struggled for breath. He glanced at the spotlight and sank onto one knee in front of her.

Oh, God. 'Get up!' It was half-sob, half-plea.

'Ava Lange…'

'Dan, please. What are you doing?' Panic had her clench-
ing icy fingers together. Her wild eyes flicked around the room.

'I just committed professional suicide rather than lose you.
Declared my love for you live on national television. Can you
possibly *not* know what I'm about to do?'

'Say yes, Ava!' someone shouted from beyond the light.

Her heart flipped into her throat.

'Ava Lange. Will you marry me and let me spend the rest of
my life loving you and apologising for what an idiot I've been?'

She sucked in a breath, speechless. Completely petrified.
Love! Facing Dione Leeds had nothing on this moment of
absolute terrifying fantasy-come-true.

He took her hand. 'If you say no, you'll be condemning me
to a lifetime of meaningless miserable encounters with Brant
Maddox cast-offs. Is that what you want?'

She wanted desperately to laugh, to lighten the moment. But
she couldn't find it in her. 'No.'

Dan blinked. Shocked. 'Wait…is that a no?'

The room went suddenly quiet. Or was it in her mind? 'No.
It's not a no.'

A huge, sexy smile spread across his face. 'So it's a yes?'

Ava looked into those dark eyes, burning with such intensity, and—*sigh*—there it was…the melted-chocolate colour of
love. Promising the world. Promising for ever. The man she'd
loved for half her lifetime.

Was there any question? Relief washed over her. And joy.
Her face split into a brilliant smile. 'Yes.'

Someone whooped at a table nearby, and in the control
booth someone hit 'play' on a loud piece of music that took the
broadcast to a well-overdue commercial break.

Dan surged to his feet, hauling Ava close, and wrapped her

in the protective circle of his arms. It was as close to privacy as they were going to get as his lips found hers. The kiss went on for eternity, leaving her oblivious to everything but the feel and taste of the wonderful man in her arms.

'People are watching,' she gasped as soon as they broke for air.

'Don't care.' He kissed her again.

She laughed against his lips. 'We've made such a spectacle.'

'Do you think anyone will remember the other story now?'

Ava pulled free and looked at him, fingers of fear skimming over her. 'Is that why you—?'

He silenced her with his mouth, then walked her backwards, out into the bright foyer, and let the huge doors swing shut on the rest of the world. He grabbed her hand. 'Quick—before they all start streaming out for the break.'

They sprinted, hand in hand, for distant doors that revealed a long hallway leading to the hotel's kitchen. Ignoring the surprise of the chefs and serving staff who glanced up, Dan scanned the room and then tugged Ava towards a comfortably large linen store.

'Perfect,' he said, barring the door behind them with an ornate candlestick across the handles.

'Dan, we can't—!'

'Shut up and kiss me.'

This kiss lasted minutes rather than seconds. She was breathless and tingly when Dan reluctantly withdrew his lips from hers and lifted his head. Everything felt like a fuzzy dream.

'I won't hold you to it, Ava. You can pull out if you want to.'

Pull out? Was he mad? Marrying Dan was everything she hadn't known she wanted. She snuggled closer in his arms. 'I wouldn't have pegged you as someone to breach a verbal agreement, Mr Arnot.'

He smiled a little nervously. 'I put you on the spot in there, Ms Lange. I wouldn't blame you.'

'I would. I'm not pulling out. And I won't let you, either.' She reached up and dragged him close for another searing kiss.

When she spoke again she was decidedly breathless. 'It's taken me too long to catch you.'

'Did you hear everything I said?' He pulled her into a strong hug, his hands roaming over the low-cut back of her dress.

'The whole country did.'

'I meant it, Ava. I will do whatever it takes to undo the damage I've caused.'

'I was coming to find you,' she whispered against his ear. 'Right before your award was read out. But Dione Leeds found me first.'

Dan pushed her away to look deep into her eyes, concerned. 'What happened?'

'Well… I seem to have made rather a good speech of my own.'

His smile fairly dazzled her. 'That's my girl.' He kissed her again, before remembering. 'Why were you looking for me?'

'I wanted to apologise. I overreacted on the dance floor—didn't give you a chance to explain. Brant helped me to realise you've been trying to protect me and your job at the same time.'

'Brant did?'

'He knows better than anyone how fine a line deception is to tread. I think he knew what you were trying to do. I should have too, and I'm sorry I doubted you.'

Dan thought that through. 'Maybe he *is* as smart as you say.' His eyes grew serious. 'I'm sorry I've kept you at arm's distance, Ava. I've held onto my hatred for so long it's become part of me.'

'Can you share it with me? Can I take some of it from you?'

He closed his eyes and rested his forehead against hers. 'Would you?'

'In a heartbeat.'

He was silent for moments. 'He was a miserable man, my father. Literally and figuratively. When my mother left he took his anger towards her out on me. I reminded him too much of her. When I was smaller he used words—emotional blackmail, verbal abuse. I'd already lost my mother, and he threatened every day to leave me, too.'

He cleared his throat and took a deep breath. Ava's hand tightened on his.

'It worked for years. That and the denigration. When I got bigger, and the words bounced off, he started in with the physical abuse. That's when your parents stepped in. Sometimes my dad didn't even notice I hadn't been home for days. He called me a no-hoper. A loser. As faithless as my mother.'

'Oh, Dan...'

His arms tightened around her. His voice was pure gravel. 'Hating her nearly killed me, Ava. But hating him saved me. It gave me purpose and courage. I channelled that into my surfing, and later my studies. I burned to prove him wrong. It was like air for me. I lived with him, so I understand why she had to leave. But I'll never understand how she could have left her little boy behind with him. Unprotected.'

Ava buried her face in his neck.

'Hey...' He stroked her hair. 'No tears. I just want you to know what kind of competition you were working against then. Even now. That nothing I did was done lightly.'

Ava dragged her mouth over his, tasting her own tears. 'I understand. I'm so sorry.'

'It was never my intention to portray you as you have been. To impact on your credibility. I know how important that is to you. Kurtz didn't like it when I refused to play along. Unfortunately, you bore the brunt of his fear of me.'

'Fear?'

'I'm better than he is. I'm better than all of them. And they know it.'

Ava smiled. 'Lord, I love that confidence.' She looked him right in the eye. 'And I love you.'

He crushed his mouth to hers and groaned. 'I never want you to stop saying that.'

'I said it nine years ago,' she mumbled against his shoulder, where she rested her head.

'Nine years ago I was so deep in the abyss I couldn't see past my own selfish needs. But even back then I recognised your feelings. I thought it would hurt less ultimately.'

She nodded, remembering how very, very much it had hurt. 'The severed limb.'

'Except you were more like a phantom limb. Even after I'd gone I still felt you. Your complete, unwavering love. It was in every story Steve told. It was in every conversation I didn't have with your father. I grew to hate that love because of what it said about me. That I could walk away like that from someone who'd offered me their heart.'

She stared at him. Resolute. Steady. 'Do you remember what you said to me that night?'

He winced. 'Which part of it?'

'"I will never be with you."'

His eyes dropped. Clouded.

'I took that with me everywhere I went, Dan. For years.' He opened his mouth to speak, but Ava pressed her fingers to his lips. 'Knowing how that one comment affected me for years after, I can't even imagine how an entire childhood of putdowns and abandonment must have impacted on you. It's a miracle you've come out a decent human being at all.'

'You can thank your father for that.' He kissed the top of her head. 'And yourself.'

'Me?'

'I may have been staggering around in my own personal morass, but I knew exactly where my light sources were. You. Your father. Even Steve. And your mother, for the short time I had her.'

Ava tucked her arms around him, holding on tight. 'You've lost two mothers.'

'But I've found true love. Not a bad consolation prize.'

Ava's hand flew to her mouth. 'You proposed to me.'

He smiled, pulling her close. 'I sure did.'

She pushed away, her hands on his chest, and looked at him meaningfully. 'Dan, listen. You proposed to me. We're getting married.'

He blinked at her, and she spelled it out for him in small words.

'My father *is* your father now.'

All the blood drained from his face, and then flushed back up in a rush. His jaw clenched and his eyes glittered with sudden moisture. Ava had never seen someone handed their dream before. Her heart exploded for him.

'That's not why I—'

She cut him off by stretching up to his lips, pressing them firmly against his, giving him a second to recover his composure. 'I know. But it's another consolation prize, huh?'

His answer was to sweep her into his arms and kiss her until they were both trembling.

Minutes passed with absolutely no distance between them, until Ava surfaced, rumpled and smudged. 'Do you think there's a fire escape somewhere close by?' she said.

Her eyes must have given her away, because Dan smiled, long and seductive. He dragged his thumb along the lower ridge of her lip, repairing the evidence of his mouth's assault. 'I have no intention of leaving.'

Her stomach clenched. 'We can't possibly go back in *there*.'

He removed a dozen pins from her dishevelled hair and let the heavy locks fall naturally over her shoulders, disguising the worst of his onslaught. 'No, I think we'll leave Kurtz to talk his way out of this one.'

'Then what?'

'I was thinking…' His hands roamed her body. 'I just got engaged to the most beautiful and brilliant woman I know, and we're standing in the linen store of the best hotel in Sydney.' He kissed her throat softly and whispered into her ear, 'And it appears my schedule is now unexpectedly clear.'

Ava giggled. 'Dan, I have no clothes with me!'

'You won't need them.' His lips trailed over her shoulder. 'Except those shoes. You'll need to keep those on.'

Her laugh turned sexy, and she dragged one of her three-inch heels up the length of his calf. 'Gosh. What would my father say?'
'He'd say *about bloody time*.'

EPILOGUE

'SHE'S loving it! Look at her.'

Ava snuggled into Dan's chest as they lay sprawled on his enormous couch, watching the widescreen TV across the room. On it, Brant and Cadence hammed it up for the cameras at an official AusOne party across town, celebrating the launch of the third season of *Urban Nature*—still Australia's most popular lifestyle programme. Brant looked gorgeous, as always, tall and tanned, and flirting shamelessly with the female half of the crowd.

Cadence—resplendent in a black creation with torn shards of PVC all over it, and three-storey buckle boots—glowered and pouted and brought new meaning to the word *surly*. The cameras ate it up.

'I just thought it would be nice if they could go to the movies together from time to time,' Ava laughed. 'I didn't expect her to become the media's darling.'

'She's a born extrovert.' Dan chuckled against her nape before pressing his lips to it. 'You don't dress like that if you're hoping *not* to be noticed.'

Dan and Cadence had established a strangely warm friendship, considering Dan had outed her on national television. She was every bit as sharp as Brant, and her quick mind and good business sense had struck a chord with Dan. Besides, he'd found himself with a vacancy for the position of honorary little sister.

'She looks happy.'

Dan laughed outright. 'What do you get that from? The freaky stare, the grim mouth, or the hostile body language?'

'Come on—look at them. He hasn't left her side. Look how he's letting her shine. Only a man deeply in love would take a back seat to his woman. She's waited a long time for that chance…'

Dan moved against her, his lips pressing harder against her nape. 'Speaking of waiting a long time…'

Ava switched off the remote and Brant and Cadence vanished. 'Don't you have some work to do?' she laughed. 'Come on, Mister Executive Producer. You owe X-Dream Sports. They saved your butt, putting you in charge of their surfing channel.' *Programming that Dan had pushed to number one in Australia.* She glanced over to where Old Faithful was propped in the hall. Back in the water after a decade. Where they both belonged.

'And you saved my butt by marrying me.' He reached around to stroke her. She wriggled against him, scrambling free.

'Seriously. You have a deadline, and so do I. I have to finish the Becher's design by Wednesday. I've got three more on the wait-list.'

Dan sighed. 'Okay. But not an all-nighter, eh? I want to watch you sleep.'

'Stalker.' Ava straightened her skirt and blouse as she stood.

'Tease.' Dan scooted out of her way, heading for his den.

Ava opened the door that joined the two parts of their home. Predictably, AusOne had repossessed her Winnebago almost immediately following the debacle of the awards night. Fortunately Steve had had the good sense to strip it of everything of Ava's while she and Dan were holed up in the Milana, on their five-day retreat from the world.

Thank goodness for big brothers.

The entire guest house was now Ava's office space. Stunning designs littered the surfaces, decorated the walls—all commissions which had come in since that disastrous story went to print and Dan's spectacular proposal at the awards.

All publicity *was* good publicity, as it turned out, and there'd been no lasting damage done to Ava's design reputation. Thanks to Dan. He'd taken a huge risk, but it had paid off. He truly was savvy when it came to the fickle entertainment industry.

Ava stretched, then sat at her angled drafting desk and pulled a blank sheet of paper over to try some new ideas. She'd barely lifted a pen before she heard the door open behind her. A moment later large, warm hands slid around her middle and soft, firm lips found her ear.

She smiled. 'What happened to working, Mr Arnot?'

'I missed you, Mrs Arnot.' His hands gently brought her to her feet. Ava's eyes fluttered closed as she felt Dan's lips move against the side of her throat, his hard body pressed against hers from behind.

'But X-Dream…?'

Dan slid his hands down her arms and took her hands in his. He whispered against her ear. 'X-Dream get me for ten hours a day. You get me for the rest.'

Ava felt the rush of excitement that always came when Dan was close. Followed closely by the deep, satisfying bond they shared. She twisted in his arms, slid her hand up under his shirt, and loved him.

* * * * *

*Rancher Ramsey Westmoreland's temporary cook
is way too attractive for his liking.
Little does he know Chloe Burton came to his ranch
with another agenda entirely....*

That man across the street had to be, without a doubt, the most handsome man she'd ever seen.

Chloe Burton's pulse beat rhythmically as he stopped to talk to another man in front of a feed store. He was tall, dark and every inch of sexy—from his Stetson to the well-worn leather boots on his feet. And from the way his jeans and Western shirt fit his broad muscular shoulders, it was quite obvious he had everything it took to separate the men from the boys. The combination was enough to corrupt any woman's mind and had her weakening even from a distance. Her body felt flushed. It was hot. Unsettled.

Over the past year the only male who had gotten her time and attention had been the e-mail. That was simply pathetic, especially since now she was practically drooling simply at the sight of a man. Even his stance—both hands in his jeans pockets, legs braced apart, was a pose she would carry to her dreams.

And he was smiling, evidently enjoying the conversation being exchanged. He had dimples, incredibly sexy dimples in not one but both cheeks.

"What are you staring at, Clo?"

Chloe nearly jumped. She'd forgotten she had a lunch date. She glanced over the table at her best friend from college, Lucia Conyers.

"Take a look at that man across the street in the blue shirt, Lucia. Will he not be perfect for Denver's first issue of *Simply Irresistible* or what?" Chloe asked with so much excitement she almost couldn't stand it.

She was the owner of *Simply Irresistible*, a magazine for today's up-and-coming woman. Their once-a-year Irresistible

Man cover, which highlighted a man the magazine felt deserved the honor, had increased sales enough for Chloe to open a Denver office.

When Lucia didn't say anything but kept staring, Chloe's smile widened. "Well?"

Lucia glanced across the booth at her. "Since you asked, I'll tell you what I see. One of the Westmorelands—Ramsey Westmoreland. And yes, he'd be perfect for the cover, but he won't do it."

Chloe raised a brow. "He'd get paid for his services, of course."

Lucia laughed and shook her head. "Getting paid won't be the issue, Clo—Ramsey is one of the wealthiest sheep ranchers in this part of Colorado. But everyone knows what a private person he is. Trust me—he won't do it."

Chloe couldn't help but smile. The man was the epitome of what she was looking for in a magazine cover and she was determined that whatever it took, he would be it.

"Umm, I don't like that look on your face, Chloe. I've seen it before and know exactly what it means."

She watched as Ramsey Westmoreland entered the store with a swagger that made her almost breathless. She *would* be seeing him again.

Look for Silhouette Desire's
HOT WESTMORELAND NIGHTS by Brenda Jackson,
available March 9 wherever books are sold.

Silhouette Desire

THE WESTMORELANDS

NEW YORK TIMES
bestselling author

BRENDA JACKSON

HOT WESTMORELAND NIGHTS

Ramsey Westmoreland knew better than to lust after the hired help. But Chloe, the new cook, was just so delectable. Though their affair was growing steamier, Chloe's motives became suspicious. And when he learned Chloe was carrying his child this Westmoreland Rancher had to choose between pride or duty.

Available March 2010 wherever books are sold.

Always Powerful, Passionate and Provocative.

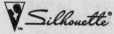

LARGER-PRINT BOOKS!

GET 2 FREE LARGER-PRINT NOVELS PLUS

2 FREE GIFTS!

From the Heart, For the Heart

YES! Please send me 2 FREE LARGER-PRINT Harlequin® Romance novels and my 2 FREE gifts (gifts are worth about $10). After receiving them, if I don't wish to receive any more books, I can return the shipping statement marked "cancel." If I don't cancel, I will receive 6 brand-new novels every month and be billed just $4.34 per book in the U.S. or $4.99 per book in Canada. That's a saving of almost 17% off the cover price! It's quite a bargain! Shipping and handling is just 50¢ per book in the U.S. and 75¢ per book in Canada.* I understand that accepting the 2 free books and gifts places me under no obligation to buy anything. I can always return a shipment and cancel at any time. Even if I never buy another book from Harlequin, the two free books and gifts are mine to keep forever.

186 HDN E4HN   386 HDN E4HY

Name	(PLEASE PRINT)	
Address		Apt. #
City	State/Prov.	Zip/Postal Code

Signature (if under 18, a parent or guardian must sign)

Mail to the **Harlequin Reader Service:**
IN U.S.A.: P.O. Box 1867, Buffalo, NY 14240-1867
IN CANADA: P.O. Box 609, Fort Erie, Ontario L2A 5X3

Not valid for current subscribers to Harlequin Romance Larger-Print books.

Are you a current subscriber to Harlequin Romance books and want to receive the larger-print edition? Call 1-800-873-8635 today!

* Terms and prices subject to change without notice. Prices do not include applicable taxes. N.Y. residents add applicable sales tax. Canadian residents will be charged applicable provincial taxes and GST. Offer not valid in Quebec. This offer is limited to one order per household. All orders subject to approval. Credit or debit balances in a customer's account(s) may be offset by any other outstanding balance owed by or to the customer. Please allow 4 to 6 weeks for delivery. Offer available while quantities last.

Your Privacy: Harlequin Books is committed to protecting your privacy. Our Privacy Policy is available online at www.eHarlequin.com or upon request from the Reader Service. From time to time we make our lists of customers available to reputable third parties who may have a product or service of interest to you. If you would prefer we not share your name and address, please check here. ☐

Help us get it right—We strive for accurate, respectful and relevant communications. To clarify or modify your communication preferences, visit us at www.ReaderService.com/consumerchoice.

HRLP10

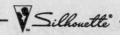

SPECIAL EDITION

FROM *USA TODAY* BESTSELLING AUTHOR
CHRISTINE RIMMER

BRAVO FAMILY TIES

A BRIDE FOR JERICHO BRAVO

Marnie Jones had long ago buried her wild-child impulses and opted to be "safe," romantically speaking. But one look at born rebel Jericho Bravo and she began to wonder if her thrill-seeking side was about to be revived. Because if ever there was a man worth taking a chance on, there he was, right within her grasp....

*Available in March
wherever books are sold.*

Love Inspired®
SUSPENSE
RIVETING INSPIRATIONAL ROMANCE

Morgan Alexandria moved to Virginia to escape her past...but her past isn't ready to let her go. Thanks to her ex-husband's shady dealings, someone's after her and, if it weren't for Jackson Sharo, she might already be dead. But can Morgan trust the former big-city cop?

HEROES *for* HIRE

RUNNING *for* COVER
by *Shirlee McCoy*

Available March wherever books are sold.

Steeple Hill®

www.SteepleHill.com

LIS44384